Kathi S. Barton

WCP

World Castle Publishing, LLC
Pensacola, Florida

Copyright © Kathi S. Barton 2014
Print ISBN: 9781629891880
eBook ISBN: 9781629891897
First Edition World Castle Publishing, LLC, December 19, 2014
http://www.worldcastlepublishing.com

Licensing Notes

Cover: Karen Fuller
Editor: Eric Johnston
Editor: Maxine Bringenberg

CHAPTER 1

Phillip moved along the inside of the cave slowly. The landslide had rendered the humans' ability to get in almost impossible. But once he and his brothers were able to shift, moving between the small openings was hard but not as impossible. Plus, their innate ability to smell the hurt or sometimes the dead was making quicker work of it.

Before he took another step inside to shift again, someone appeared in front of him. She pressed her finger to her lips, which silenced the question he'd nearly asked her about whether she was hurt or needed to come with him. She was dressed in a dark neoprene outfit that fit her skin like it had been painted on her. There were weapons all over her body, as well as a large Glock in her hand. He nodded once to it, and she smiled. Then when she lifted her hand up and spread her fingers, he watched as she brought it to her face.

As she looked at him through her spread fingers, he had an idea she was trying to tell him something but refrained from asking. Instead he watched as she pulled her still spread fingers from her face and put her hand in front of her mouth in a speaking motion. Phillip was still confused until she put her spread fingers in front of his face about five or six inches away. He got it then and nodded. But she still held her hand there, and he had a feeling he had to okay her touching him by putting his face in her hand. Leaning forward, for whatever reason trusting her, she curved her fingers over his face once he was there and touched him.

Her pinkie and thumb touched his ears. Then her fingers next to those touched his eyes as her middle finger dug into his scalp. It wasn't painful, but he could feel her probing his mind just a little. Before he could move back, even if he thought he could, she pulled her hand away and he staggered back.

I'm not going to hurt you. He looked at her, and she smiled again. *You're not who I was looking for but you'll have to do. The leader of you, where is he?*

I think he's coming in from the north side. He and my other brothers have split up to make this faster. These people have been in here for over twenty hours. She nodded and looked to his left. Another man, dressed as she was, stood there looking at them both, and he was armed as well. When he put up his hand, as the woman had, he simply moved into it to speak to him as well.

I'm Nic, and this is my sister. We're here to find a rogue. He might have been the cause of all this mess. Phillip didn't say anything, but did notice that while he was armed as well, the woman had put her gun away. *We don't really need your help, but we can make this easier on you. Once you're doing what you need to do, we can get on with our job and you and yours won't get hurt. This is not a safe place for any of us, especially you guys.*

I'll give you a map in your head to find all the people left in here. There are twenty-seven, not counting the one we're looking for. Nine are dead; I will show you where they are as well. But the man we want for our own. Phillip was already shaking his head at the woman as she took over for Nic. *You won't deal with us?*

I will if Misha approves. But I'm thinking it will take too long. What is the deal?

She smiled at her brother, then looked at him. Phillip had a feeling that they were communicating with each other, and he was suddenly a little nervous.

Misha Lanning? He nodded. *He won't deal with us unless he covers every avenue and has a contract in his hand saying what will need to be given and taken. Your people don't have time for that. I can just go and get my guy, leave you guys here fumbling in the dark while others die, or you let me do what I want and you get to be a hero.*

I'm not really the hero type. She laughed in his head, and he smiled. He had no idea why he thought he could trust either of them, but he did. *All right, but if he asks me what the hell you're doing here, I'm going to tell him straight up you made me do it.*

She put out her hand and smiled. *Deal. I'll get my man, you'll get the others out. I'll give you a way to find them, and you'll...well, you're going to need help with some of the areas. There are stones falling everywhere.*

The mountain above them took a sudden jerk, and she reached for him. He was sure she was helping him, but a need to protect her had him covering her with his body. For only about two seconds. Then he found himself not only covered by her, but by the man as well.

When he was pulled to his feet, he could see that the huge rock that had fallen had hit her. Phillip looked at the stone and knew that had they not protected him when they did, he'd be dead. Her suit was torn, and a big gash had been torn into her flesh as well. She waved Nic off, but Phillip could tell she was in pain.

Here's what you're going to need. She touched her finger to his head, and he felt as if he'd been shocked with an electrical current...and he saw a map form in his head. *The red areas are the most dangerous, the blue is where the living are, and the green is where the dead are. The places that are circled in the red are where you're going to need help. I would avoid the red areas altogether if I was you.*

And where are you going? He didn't expect her to answer him, and she didn't. When Nic moved ahead of them, she turned back to him again.

You should really not tell anyone we were in here with you. We're sort of...well, we're not really a group of people you want to piss off.

What are you? She looked down the way her brother had gone, then back at him. She looked...well, he thought, sad for a few moments. Then anger surged forward. Before she turned to leave him, she looked back over her shoulder.

I am Genjar.

Phillip stood there for several seconds, trying to absorb what she'd said. Genjar, as in the species that had been destroyed centuries ago? He had to have heard her wrong. They were all dead, he thought. But if she was telling him the truth, and he had no idea why she'd lie to him about that, he thought maybe he knew why they didn't want anyone to know they'd been there. When she touched his mind again, he had to laugh.

Mull it over later, Phillip Lanning. There are bodies to find, and you standing there thinking things through isn't going to get them out. He reached for his brothers, looking over the map she'd given him. *I'll go and talk to your leader when I'm sure you're not going to tell them we were here. If you do, you and your entire family will die before the next sunrise. Understand?*

Phillip told her he did, and decided that other than telling Misha and making him understand what the hell was going on, he'd never tell anyone. But damn, he'd just met a Genjar.

Thomas reached him first, then Carter and Misha. Rider was on his way, as was Andrew, but they were making their way through the landslide looking for others as he made his way out and back around. Phillip told him he knew just where they were and to come now. He was the youngest of the brothers, but he knew when he said he had information, they'd come faster. He then reached for Misha as they stood there in the opening.

I have the information that we need to get them all out. Misha raised a brow at him but said nothing. *I had help, and she said she'd talk to you later. We can't tell anyone she and her brother were here.*

And why is that? He didn't answer him, and Misha stopped him from moving toward the first area. *And why is it you can't tell me or anyone else who she was?*

Because if I do, she'll kill us. Misha stood there for several seconds before he nodded. One thing about his brother, he could read people like a book, and he would know if anyone was lying to him. So when they got to the first area, the one that had several of the living inside, they worked together and got five of the living out, including a newborn. There was one dead among them. He was helping to pull the living ones to safer ground when he heard from the woman again.

Our rogue is on the move. We will protect you as best we can, but you're not to engage. If you do, he will kill you.

Phillip relayed the information from the woman to Misha. Misha told them to stand down. When a flash ran by them, the rogue he supposed, the man never even looked their way. But Phillip did tell the woman and Nic where he was headed.

Thank you. I owe you one.

The work was slow going in the red area. They managed to just save their asses when the earth moved again, bringing down a mountain, it seemed, of mud and mire. They were able to get out all of the living and the eight dead in a quarter of the time it would have taken without the help of the Genjar.

Misha was standing in front of the police officer talking to him when Nic touched Phillip's mind again.

My sister is hurt, and it will be several days before she can see your brother. Could you have him set her an appointment for Tuesday a week from now? I know that she will say sooner, but I'd appreciate it if you'd simply tell her it was the best you can do. Phillip laughed and told him he was more afraid of her than him. *As well you should be. If you know anything about our kind, you know the women are the strongest. You will do as she asks then, and I will see if I can hold her off. She is most...stubborn.*

Phillip thought that was an understatement but didn't say anything else. Instead he watched Misha as he walked to the news crew that was waiting for information.

"We believe, by a counting of what the police have gathered, that all the victims are accounted for. The dead were moved to a safe location, and the injured are at the local stations set up to transport if necessary. The good news is, there was one more person within the slide than we had been told of." Misha waited for the crews to stop shouting questions, and Phillip thought for sure that he was going to tell about the rogue. "One of the victims gave birth to her daughter, and both of them are doing well. They have been sent to the hospital for observation. The people with her deserve a pat on the back for not only helping her when she needed it, but also keeping them both safe until we could get to them."

Misha walked away and toward him. Phillip knew he was upset but not about what. When he went to the car they'd rented to get there, the rest of them followed. There was no reason for them to hang around and they rarely did. But Phillip was a little leery of getting in the big car with his pissed off brother. The rest of them got into the other two vehicles.

"Tell me what you know of this woman and her brother. And I mean everything. Did you know that there was no listing for whoever they were looking for? For all we know they doctored the manifest up and took someone they were hired to kill." Phillip wanted to reach for Nic to tell him it was a good time to have the meeting, but the man appeared. He smiled at Phillip, then put out his hand to Misha.

"You are the leader to this leap?" Misha nodded and took his hand. "Good. My sister is indisposed at the moment. We were looking for a rogue that simply would not cooperate with us. But we have him now and he is being brought to justice. I'm Nic."

"So?" Nic laughed at Misha. "What did this rogue do that someone had to be sent to find him now? Did you know we might have given you a hand in catching him?"

"No. You would have hindered us." Misha started to speak, but Nic continued. "He was as we are, yet he had been using his magic for things that are best left unsaid. The slide was his doing to cover his tracks of a heinous murder. You were very lucky that we happened upon your family before he did. He does not play well with others."

"Neither do I." Misha leaned back on the seat while the driver continued on as if there wasn't a new person in the car with them. "What are you? And if you give me some bullshit answer, I'll make your life a living hell."

Nic looked at Phillip and then back at Misha. "You have a very loyal brother here. I would have thought he'd tell you what my sister told him. He is much more trustworthy than I first thought. We are the Genjar, and we have been hiding for many years. From the look on your face, I would say you are well aware of what we can do."

"You're all dead." Nic laughed, and Misha flushed. "I'm sorry. That came out harsh. What I meant to say is that—"

"We want people to think we're dead for now. It serves us better this way. Young Phillip here, he was told not to say a word and as a man of honor, I can only assume you are as well." Misha looked at him before Nic continued. "Or is it your mother that rules the leap?"

"She does. As does my wife." Misha laughed when Nic did. "You and your sister, are you the only ones left of your kind?"

"Nay, we are not. There are a great many of us. Not as many as we once were, but enough to make a nice showing if we needed to." Nic looked out the window. "We are headed to the airport?"

"Yes. We never hang around when things are settled. It takes a great deal out of us all when we do search and rescue like this." Nic nodded. "Are you coming with us?"

"Nay, not this time. My sister has been injured and I would like to make sure she rests. It will be most difficult to make her do so, but I can only try. She would like a meeting with you soon. Sooner than I would like, but soon." Misha nodded. "May I ask that your family be present as well? We have formed a bond with your brother Phillip here, and would like to extend the same to the rest of the leap."

"I think I can arrange that." Nic nodded. "How will she contact me? I'm assuming it won't be by conventional means."

"Not with her. You're not going to…my sister can be a bit of a bitch when the mood suits her. Which is most of the time. But she will contact young Phillip here. She had a connection with him that will serve until we can meet. My parents will be there as well. And I would ask that you make arrangements for them to stay somewhere close. They love to travel and have never been to this part of the world before."

"They are welcome in our home." Nic nodded and turned to Phillip. He put out his hand again, this time in the form of a handshake, and Phillip took it.

"Until we meet again."

Then he was gone. Misha stared at Phillip for several minutes before he spoke. Phillip wasn't sure what to expect but was going to take it. He'd kept something from his leader and his brother, and he knew that Misha would be pissed.

"You knew what they were before?" Phillip nodded. "Then you did the right thing. Knowing what they were might have made me…I don't know, but you can bet that it wouldn't have gone well for us. Or the people we were there to save."

"She was hurt saving my ass when a slide landed on me. I don't know if she was hurt again or not, but it looked bad." Misha nodded. "Are you pissed at me?"

"No. On the contrary, I'm very proud of you. It must have been difficult for you not to tell me. Especially when I demanded. You did well." Misha looked at him then. "But don't tell the family just yet. It would be better that we don't. Just in case Nic and his family decide not to come."

Phillip nodded but had a feeling they'd show up. And when they did, it was going to be fireworks. He had no idea, but he thought the mother was going to be just as stubborn as the daughter. Then he realized he'd never gotten her name. Phillip had a feeling that was planned too.

~~~

Linyah wanted to scream, but she knew if she did, they'd never let her out of the hospital. The pain wasn't getting any better and she was getting to the point where she wanted to tell them to leave her the fuck alone. When Nic walked into the room with her, she glared at him.

"It will do you no good to look at me as if I did this to you. I did warn you he was coming toward you." She glared harder. "Shall I tell you of my meeting with the leap leader? He was most...I do believe I would like this man a great deal."

"You went to see him without me?" She tried to sit up, but the woman standing next to her pushed her back down. She looked at the doctor, then the man who was helping her. Linyah thought he looked nervous, scared even, but he turned away before she could ask what was wrong. Instead she let her anger vent on her brother. "You want to live a little longer, I'd tell me what you know. I'm not in the mood for you to be treating me like I'm five." Pain shot through her back that took her breath away, and she glared at the doctor. Her smile was not comforting, and she told the woman to hurry the fuck up.

"Yes, ma'am." She moved back so quickly that she bumped into the table behind her. Linyah felt marginally better. Then she looked at Nic.

"What did he say? And why did you go to see him without me?" Nic stretched out his legs as the attendants in the room scrambled to leave. She had a feeling he'd told them to get out. He would have been a great deal politer than she.

"He was pissed at young Phillip. And by the way, you were most right about him. He didn't tell who we were, not even when his brother commanded him to do so." She nodded, knowing that he wouldn't, but was glad he had done what she'd asked. "I interceded on his behalf, as I'm sure you would have done had you been able to."

"He saved our ass, you know." Nic nodded. "When the rogue knocked me down, we were headed in the wrong direction. I'm glad we trusted him."

"As am I. Also, before we get out of here and into where everyone can hear us, I've invited our parents along with us when we go and meet the leap. I do believe that Misha and Father will get along very well. And his mother, from what I could gather about her in his mind, would suit Mother as well." She nodded, knowing that even if she objected they'd come along anyway. "You should also know that Misha is a great deal like our sister Kendra. A leader with more than just a little temperament to go with it."

"You're saying he's a bitch too and that he'll hate me." Nic told her for probably the millionth time that their sister didn't hate her. Changing the subject because she knew better, she looked around the room. "We'll go as soon as I'm able. But Nic, that man…he hurt me. I'm not used to being on the receiving end of this much pain."

"He did. Let me see the damage, love." She lifted her gown up when he asked her to. "He did indeed. I should like for you to rest for at least a few days, Linyah. You will need your strength to deal with the leap, and I'd rather you weren't injured should we be needed again. Besides, I think if you try to leave here, Kendra will be most displeased with you. She thinks…I have told her that you were injured, as I should, and she might come to see you."

Linyah lay back on the bed and nodded. "She'll come. What would she be as a leader of this clan if she didn't? I should have listened to you. You said he was armed. And I'll never admit this, but you were right, too, about me needing more practice when it comes to my demanding people do as I say. I should have asked first."

Nic stood up and pulled her gown up higher. She'd hoped that he'd not notice that she'd been cut more than what she'd shown him. He only looked her in the eye before sitting back down.

"Your back as well?" She nodded. "And when were you going to tell me of this? You are my baby sister and I love you. You are not going to be able to do this forever if you continue to take such chances."

"I will live forever, same as you. But you're right. I need to take better care. Maybe someday you'll find yourself a female to breed with. Then I can see how bad it is having one and I might find me one as well. Just so he can heal me. No other reason." He stood up, laughing. "You think I'd want someone like you ordering me around like I'm a simpleton?"

"I would never think you'd find a male to love you if you did not want it. But I do believe there are more pleasures to having a male in your life than simply to put you back together." He kissed her forehead as he made his way to the door. "Take care, sister. I do need you around a bit longer."

She lay back on the bed and waited for the idiots to come in. All they could do to help her was clean the wounds, then stitch them together and nothing more. No one could heal her, and even though her kind could heal others, they could never heal themselves. If they did, they would die. And it would be a horrific death.

Linyah had never been afraid at her job before. Never in all the centuries she'd done it, but today she had been. And not only that, she'd fucked up. Badly. Her mind had been elsewhere and not on what she should have been doing. She'd been thinking of the young man Phillip and whether she'd made a huge mistake in giving him a little of herself. But talking with Nic, she knew now it had been a good thing. And he'd saved them from having to explain to the authorities what had happened about the one that had killed so many. Including today's count.

The man had gotten by Nic, and she'd been stupid enough to think she could take him on her own. Stupidity had nearly gotten her cut to ribbons too, had it not been for Nic coming to her aid. She'd been so stunned by the pain he'd inflicted on her from his magic that she'd dropped to the floor rather than fight back. Blinded by it, she nearly forgot to warn the others in the slide and had only just gotten the message to young Phillip. It was a good thing, too, because she'd been leading them away from the rogue rather than toward him. Now the man was in custody and set to be killed. It was a good day.

"Have you decided to live then?" She looked up at her sister and frowned. "I'm glad to see that you're at least letting them put you back together this time rather than me having to come down here and put you to sleep again. I'm most unhappy when I have to do that to you."

"As am I." The others, who had come back in when Nic had gone, left, but this time it was because they'd done all they could for her. "We're going to go on a trip. To some leopards that helped us out today. Do you think Mother and Father will go?"

"So I have heard. And I think keeping them away will be next to impossible. I have heard of this man, Misha Lanning. He will be a good ally to have. You have met him then?" She shook her head and told her that Nic had. "Nic says we are to be settled in his home. I should like that. But I think...this will upset you, but I believe it would be better if you were to stay here. It will give you time to—"

"No." Her sister, queen now that Mother had retired, only glared at her. "I've been the one in contact with this family. I should go. They saved us, saved me from being too hurt."

"You mean more than you are now?" Linyah nodded. "I have already decided, and you will do as I have said. It will be better for all concerned if you were to stay here and get better. I do not want you to get weaker."

So it was settled. Linyah settled back on the bed and closed her eyes when her sister left. She knew that resting would speed the process up, but nothing would get her better overnight. And now that she was forbidden to go on the trip, there was really no reason whatsoever for her to stay tied to this bed. She'd heal when she healed. She knew that she would heal faster if she took a male, which she was never going to do. "Not ever." Just before falling into a sound sleep, she thought about finding Nic a female, and smiled. He was going to hate her for doing it, and it was all the more reason for her to do it.

CHAPTER 2

The house was in a shambles, and Thomas couldn't stand it. He liked neat and orderly, and this place was anything but. Moving out onto the deck to get away from the mess inside, he met with a bigger one there. Why were they planting so many flowers around the deck when the gardens looked like someone had run them over with a mower? He sat on the small swing and watched them scurry around like they had no idea what they were doing.

"You hate this, don't you?" He looked over at Hannah, Misha's mate, and smiled at her. "I can see you going over there and making them straighten out the rows of flowers. I'm actually surprised you haven't yet."

"I was about to, but I'm pretty sure that the foreman over there would have my head on a pike. He warned me earlier that I was to keep away from him." Thomas stood up when she sat down next to him. There was not enough room for him to sit with her and not touch her. "Misha said they are to arrive in two days. I guess you'll be entertaining them for a while too."

"I suppose. Do you have any idea where they're coming from? Misha said that he never thought to ask, only that they'd need a place to stay." Thomas shook his head, knowing that from what Misha had said, it was another part of the world. And that they were not human. "Did you meet them? Either of them?"

"No. Phillip is the only one that met them both, and Misha only met the man. Nic, he said his name was. But no one has the name of the woman. I guess she impressed Phillip with her skills as a fighter." Thomas leaned against the railing around the deck and looked at Hannah rather than the mess in the yard. "Mom's house is ready. I can move in anytime I want."

"I wish you would stay here. You know that there is enough room for you all." He nodded but didn't say anything. "I guess Carter and Phillip are moving out too. They said they needed their space."

"Space for their women." She laughed when he smiled at her. "I guess it's time for us to be on our own. I'm really glad to be getting the old house, and it's nice that I could stay here while I had it worked on. The kitchen was nice but really outdated. And I had to have some of the rooms redone as well. The office looks very nice, thanks to you."

"All I did was give you the stuff in the building we had downtown. And Daniel and his wife, Wanda, are moving into the house at the other end of the street. I'm very glad you talked me into meeting them. I like Uncle Daniel." Thomas liked Daniel too, and his family, and he'd been really excited when Daniel was offered a job working for security for Misha and the firm. "I guess his parents aren't really happy with him or me."

Mr. and Mrs. Howard Little were Hannah's real grandparents. Her mom, Kelli Little, had been kicked out of the house when they'd found out she was pregnant and only seventeen. Later she'd been murdered and her child, Hannah, had been taken from her by a woman who had abused and nearly killed Hannah until Misha had stepped in. Life was considerably better for her now, and she was blooming now that she could see that people could love her. She still had her days when she was afraid, but they were becoming a thing of the past too.

"When are they coming, do you know?" Hannah shrugged and looked away, and his heart hurt for her. "You don't have to have them here if you don't want them to be. I'm sure that we can take care that the visit never happens. Any or all of us could take care that they never bother you again."

When she looked at him, he wiggled his brows at her, and she laughed. It was what he'd hoped for, and when she leaned back and sighed, he wanted to pull her into his arms and comfort her. She spoke before he could suggest that she go into town with his mom and have lunch.

"I want to meet them, but I don't. There is something so…I guess frightening about knowing that I have a set of grandparents out there that can be just as cruel to me as Bella had been." She looked at him. "Not in the same way, but just as cruel. Does that make sense?"

"It does." He tried to think of something to say that would lighten the mood. "These beings that are coming here, what do you know of them? Other than the fact that they helped us bring out those people. Do you suppose they'll all be here at once?"

"I hope not. And nothing really. Misha said that they're strong and that we should go out of our way to make them feel welcome. I don't know what they are, but I have a feeling that it's something huge. I heard Phillip has a connection with them both and has been talking to them. The woman—her name hasn't been said yet—has been recuperating for the past several days and I guess she won't be coming with them. Do you know what happened to her?" He told her he didn't. "I guess whatever they are, we're going to be ready for him. Misha said that he was going to have the landscaping done this fall anyway, so this is as good a time as any to get it going. I think it was fine before. But then I'm always afraid of spending money. But he assures me he has a great deal of it."

"He does. We all do." He looked behind him when a large engine roared to life. The trees they were pulling off the flatbed truck looked nearly full grown. He wondered how much more this poor yard could take. But then he could see that the men who were planting the gardens near the house were nearly finished. There was a reason to their method. He could see that now. Standing up, he watched the trees, all five of them, being put in the ground as Hannah napped. She'd been doing that a lot lately, and he wondered if she knew why.

He turned away from her, smiling. She was going to have a fit if she didn't know now that she was going to have a baby. And Misha was going to have some major explaining to do too. Thomas almost wished he was living here just for that. Instead he moved off the deck and to his car. The appliances for his kitchen should be set by now and he was excited to be there to see them. He also wanted to get started on a few other renovations that he'd thought about, one of them being the dining room.

Thomas pulled into his drive twenty minutes later and sat there looking at his home. It was the one he'd grown up in, sure, but now it was all his. He'd been doing some repairs on it, not much but enough to show that it was under new care, and he loved it. The new shutters and windows practically danced with light and color, and he loved the new wrap-around porch too. Getting out, he moved to the back of the house to enter through the kitchen and nearly bumped into his cook. His mother had hired him one while he'd been gone on the last mission with his brothers. The man was a wonder too.

"I've taken the liberty of putting you in a baked potato to go with your steak tonight. I do hope that is fine." Thomas nodded and sat at the table. The two of them had been making headway into becoming employee to employer. Today they'd actually made some ground rules. And of course, now Mike knew who and what he was working for.

"Mike, what do you suppose we could do to the dining room? It looks good, I guess, but extremely outdated like this room had been." Mike had helped him a great deal in the kitchen, and Thomas now welcomed his input on the rest of the house. His office was completely ready for him in half the time it would have been had Thomas done it himself. The man simply knew everyone, it seemed, and each of them had a talent for doing something he needed.

"You'll need a bigger room first of all. With the family growing now, you'll need a larger space for the table and chairs. Of course, some built in china cabinets will be nice too. Less walking back and forth to set up the room." Thomas and Mike Vickers moved into the next room. It was sort of smallish and he wondered how they could get more space. "I know a man who can come in and enlarge this room to about double without messing up the structure of the room. And it would fit nicely with the deck as well. Having some big doors that will spill out onto it will make the room look bigger too."

"I like it. Have him come out and look it over. Then give me an idea what he can do. And while he's here, see what he can do about the living room. I know that it's the biggest room in the house, but it needs something too. I was thinking about the fireplace. It needs revamped." Mike nodded and moved back into the kitchen when a timer went off. Thomas sat down at the table just thinking about all the meals they'd had in here as a family. Someday he'd like to have his own, just not yet. When he heard a noise at the back door, then Mike arguing, he got up to see what was going on. Mike was a laid back sort of guy, but he didn't sound that way right now.

"What do you want?"

His father was standing there like he was going to barge right in and knock the shit out of Mike. But when Thomas asked him again what he wanted, he took a step back.

"I was wanting to see your mother. She and I have to talk." Thomas nodded but didn't invite his dad in. "You pissy with me too? I had a life to live and being saddled with a bunch of kids wasn't anything I wanted at the time. Now I see you all have done well for yourselves and I thought you'd welcome me in." His dad moved to come through the closed screen door, but Thomas stepped in front of him.

"No." His dad looked confused so he explained himself, and not nicely. "No, I'm not going to invite you in. No, I'm not going to have you sponging off us now that you've decided that you'd take us back, and hell no, you're not coming near my mother. I told you before that you aren't welcome here."

"That isn't any way to talk to your father, boy. Didn't I raise you to have respect for your elders?"

Thomas laughed and his father looked like he was going to not just come in but try to knock the shit out of him as well.

"You do whatever is going on in your mind and it will be the last thing you ever do. And I mean breathing too. As for you raising us? You had nothing to do with us being the men we are. Mom did that all on her own. And if you want me to give you a lesson in having respect for someone, you go near my mother and I will tear you apart. Do I make myself clear?"

"You ain't no son of mine." Thomas couldn't have agreed more and told him so. "You see that I don't tell everyone I see what you did to your own father. Then we'll see how much respect they have for you. A man should help his father out, not turn him out like a dog. You see that this here don't come back and bite you in the ass."

"I'm not afraid of anything you do or say. Everyone in this town knows what sort of person you are and the fact that you left Mom on her own. Not ever sending money home to help her. I'm thinking that you might be surprised at just how much lack of respect you get from anyone you talk to. As for any money? You should have thought of what might have befallen you before you left us for all your fun." Thomas closed the door in his father's face and then turned to Mike. The man was staring at him like he was slightly afraid and a great deal impressed.

"I can hold dinner, sir, if you'd like to go on a run." Thomas nodded and moved through the house toward the back to where his office was that spilled out into the lawn beyond. He was nearly naked when he threw open the door and shifted in mid-leap off the deck. The run was hard and fast, and he didn't care if he ever returned to being a human.

~~~

Linyah wanted to go now. She was sick to death of waiting on someone to get their asses in gear to say this was when they were going. She was pretty sure that her parents knew when they were going, but no one was sharing with her. Linyah glared at her bed and the mess that was there.

Kendra had given her permission to go, but not without rules that she was required to follow. Linyah had gone to her dad, and he said he'd talk to Kendra. Whatever he'd said worked. To a point. Now she could go, but she wasn't allowed to get pissy, and—this one did piss her off—she had to wear a dress at least once while they were there if invited to dinner.

"You should have made it first before throwing all your clothing on it. I swear, Linyah, you are the messiest person I know." She turned to smile at her mom. "How will you know what you're taking and not taking with all your things spread out everywhere?"

"I'm taking a toothbrush, my uniforms, and a pair of underwear. I thought I could rinse them out nightly and not have to worry about them." Her mother looked horrified. "I'm kidding, Mom. And Sheda is packing for me. This is just stuff she said I wasn't going to take with me. Did you really give her a list to follow?"

"I did. I knew that you'd pack those horrid uniforms just to displease me, and I wanted them to see you as I do. A lovely woman who can dress up when the time is right. I heard your sister also had some input for that girl of yours, but like you would have done, she tossed it out.

You'll have to keep Sheda close to you for a while. I don't think your sister will harm her, but she might shift her to another estate." Her mom lifted up a long curl from her shoulder and Linyah backed away. "You will not be pulling this up into a knot atop your head either. I want them to see you for a woman, not a male. You'll never find your male if you continue to dress as one of them. Sex and men are very nicely put together."

"I'm pretty sure that anyone can tell I'm a woman even if I'm in my uniform. Not that I care what men or, for that matter, women think of me either way, but you should know that I've been seen as a woman for a long time. And men like me and my body undressed more than what I wear." Her mother flushed. "You should know better than to talk to me about men and sex."

"You are driving me crazy, did you know that?" Linyah smiled. "I have come to talk to you about something important. Nic thinks we should have an outpost on Earth. I think it a good idea, but I wanted your input before I went to your sister. She can be...difficult when the mood suits her. Why she's not more like you, I'll never know. But anyway, he thinks that if there is someone there when we have a problem, it will be quicker to deal with."

"I think it's a good idea. And if you tell Kendra that, she'll shoot it down even if it is an excellent idea. Did he say who would run it?" Her mother nodded sadly. "I see. He wants to run it. Well, he should. He'd be great at it too."

"You want him to be gone from our home? I don't think...it's the only way, I'm sure, but to have him so far away. What will I do if I need him here for something?

You know your father depends on him a great deal when you are working."

"Dad will be fine with him there. And he'd love to go there more often with you. I think you should purchase a house there as well. Something just the two of you could use to get away. That part of the world is a very...it's very different than here. You might enjoy it a little." Her mom was liking the idea and Linyah could see it. "And this Misha person might be a good friend to you both. His brother is a very strong and good man. I can only assume that he will be too."

"Nic said he is very nice. Polite too, he told us, unlike some people I know. And your dad seems to think he might be able to help us when we have a rogue or two as well. Not that you don't do a fantastic job, but it would be nice to have someone so close to the action when things go wrong." Linyah knew what she was saying was true, but she also didn't want anyone helping her. But she kept her mouth shut. It was never going to happen anyway. Her parents wouldn't buy a home there and Nic would be bored soon enough and push the outpost onto someone else. But it was a good plan. Her sister would hate it simply because Linyah had some input on it.

Her mother was walking toward the door when she turned back. "We leave in the morning for the Lanning leap. Are you going to be well enough to travel?" Tomorrow? She nodded at her mom. "Good. I will have your things taken to the transport and they will be there when we arrive. Do try to act like a woman for just the first few hours, my child. I would very much like to make a good first impression."

Linyah stuck her tongue out at the closed door. She was going to be herself and if they didn't like it, then tough shit. She wasn't going to dress up for anyone. Besides, she was pretty sure that she'd never see the Lannings again and didn't care to dress to impress. Maybe she'd get a call to go out and be on a mission until they were ready to come back here. Not that she wasn't looking forward to going, but she wasn't going to be made into something she wasn't. She reached for Phillip to tell him they were coming tomorrow morning.

Your things will be brought to my brother's house. He's got all the rooms assigned and everything all set up. I hope you like my family. She told him she didn't care about all that, and he laughed. *Yeah, I didn't think you'd care. But my mom is looking forward to you guys coming. She's been baking her famous sugar cookies and pies.*

Her downfall. Sweets. Linyah had asked the kitchen here not to bake them any longer. She could sit and eat them until she popped. And then eat more just because she could. It wasn't like she gained any weight or anything, but they did make her have such a sugar rush that it was like being drunk on liquor. She had made such a fool of herself the last time she'd eaten any that she'd had to stay at home for days in fear someone would laugh at her.

I don't know how long we'll be staying, but there is a chance that I'll get called away when a problem arises. She'd told Phillip that she was in charge of security, and he told her that was great. What she didn't tell him was that not only did she run the security team, but did most of the runs on her own. She'd been running away as far as she could since her mother retired some years ago. But Linyah was bored with the job and she was pretty sure her mother was with retirement as well. Maybe they'd all get lucky and her mom would come out of retirement and her sister would find a male. Yeah, right, she thought. And she'd turn into a beauty queen.

Whatever happens it'll be nice just to have you here as much as we can. I'm looking forward to everyone meeting you and your family. Linyah smiled. There wasn't a nicer person she knew than this young man. And she supposed that he wasn't really young to others like him. But to her he was just a babe. *Misha said we might have a call or two as well to go out on. I guess we might miss seeing you as well. There is always someone who needs us.*

Me too. She looked out over the grounds that were home to so many now. *I have seen some of your area in your mind. I hope someday that I can bring you here. It's so different than yours. We don't have a lot going on that's different than you have really. Just bigger houses and less people. I guess we're still hoping that someday we'll be as populated as we once were.* She didn't mean to sound so snobbish and started to apologize to him when he laughed.

It is okay here. I don't know where there is, but I'm sure you'll like our little piece of the world. It's nice, quiet, and we have a lot of woods we can run in. I've been telling Mom about you and she can't wait to meet you. Pressure seemed to weigh her down and she had to take several deep breaths before she could speak. But Phillip was speaking first. *You'll be fine. Just take more deep breaths and imagine fighting one of your worst foes. See him at the end of your blade? He's scared shitless of your badassness. And he'd be pissing his pants if not for the fact that you've already made him do it twice.*

Linyah laughed. She couldn't help it. He'd been making her do that so often that she wanted to find him and hug him to her. But it wasn't sexual, and she was sure he knew it. It was like he was her brother, like Nic was, and they got along so well. When she told him she was fine now, he told her he had to go. They were having a meeting again and he couldn't be late.

Linyah was sitting on her deck hours later when she realized that she wanted to be there now. Instead of telling anyone where she was going, she simply willed herself to the house where Phillip was. She was surprised to find herself in the kitchen with a large man that looked to be pissed off. The older woman that was standing in the doorway looked to be just as mad as the man, but she was also afraid. Linyah stepped between them. The older leopard turned to her and she saw the gun before anything else.

"You should just back on up, girl, and nobody will get hurt. I'm here to talk to my boy and you'll not interfere. Don't you just be standing there. Get going. Don't you have something to sew or something?" He glared at her when she laughed. "I'm not being funny here. I'm trying to be polite and I don't have a lot of politeness in me today. You just back on up and I'll finish my conversation with my wife here."

Linyah turned slightly to look at the woman. She'd been hit, and hard too. Before she could ask her if she was all right, another man came up behind the older one and wrapped his arm around his throat, pulling him away from the door. Linyah could see that he had it covered and helped the woman to sit down.

"You should have kicked his ass." Linyah laughed at the woman when she spoke. "I would have, but I'm no match for him. Stupidity makes mean men. And he's one of the meanest ones I know of."

"I'll agree with that, but I'm pretty sure you could have taken him and come out on top." Linyah touched the wound on her cheek and healed it. She knew that she could have healed herself by shifting, but she wanted to help her. "I assume you're Phillip's mother and that monster was your husband?"

"Ex-husband, thank you. And yes. I'm Maribel and you're the young woman who Phillip has been raving about since he met you." The younger man came in the door then, and she stood in front of Mrs. Lanning. He didn't move any further into the room but stared at her. "Thomas, did you kick his butt and put him in his car? He should know better than to come here."

"He said he was coming back. I called Misha and told him." He never stopped staring at Linyah as he spoke to his mom. "Phillip said he was around the main house today too. He told him not to come back. Did he hurt you?"

"Nothing she couldn't fix up with a touch." Mrs. Lanning stood up and pushed her toward the man. "Thomas, this is Phillip's friend. I'm sorry, dear, we don't know your name."

"Linyah. I'm Linyah of the Genjar people." Linyah flushed. She never told people what she was when asked, but for some reason she did now. Before she could say anything else, the man laughed. Linyah felt her anger build up.

"This day just went from good to shit in a matter of heartbeats, didn't it? I don't suppose you have a mate, do you?" She shook her head. "Of course not. That would just make it too nice and easy. I wonder what else is in store for me. Plague? The bank go belly up?"

"Thomas." His mother was shocked, that much was evident. But when she smacked him on the back of the head, he only looked at her and smiled. "Tell the young woman you're sorry. She was just saving me from being hurt by your father when you showed up."

"He's only my sire, Mom, not my father." Linyah took a step back when he took one toward her. "I need to touch you."

She took another step back, then another when he kept coming. Putting up her hands was a bad idea, she knew, so she put them behind her. Before she could leave the room and this man, he wrapped his fingers around her upper arm, causing her pain. When she cried out, he didn't let her go but pulled her into his arms and held her. Linyah didn't know what to do then.

"Thomas?" He turned them both to his mom. "Thomas, is she your mate? Is this your mate?"

No one said anything and she pulled away from him to look into his eyes. She could see it there. He thought her his mate. But before she could tell him that there was no way in hell she was his, he lowered his head and brushed his mouth over hers. Fuck, but that was wonderful. And nothing could have prepared her for the sexual need he'd given her with just a simple kiss.

Linyah pulled her mouth from his and he moved down her throat. She could see his desire, and his erection was pressed hard into her folds. She had to get away. Now. She had to get away now before he touched her again. Stepping back again, he let her go and she willed herself home. She started to throw things into another bag as she tried to think what to tell her mom.

"I'm not going." Linyah knew that would never work. Her mom would want more than just a simple statement, especially since she'd been going on and on about visiting them. And if she told her that her male was at the Lanning house, they'd be moving there as soon as it could be arranged. Linyah needed that like she needed another hole in her body. Grabbing up the bag she'd thrown together, she was out of the house before anyone noticed her. Going to the mountains was her only safe place. They couldn't find her there, nor could she be reached. Linyah was running away from home.

CHAPTER 3

"What do you mean you can't find her? She's your sister, find her." Nic wanted to point out that she was also their daughter, but didn't think that would go over well just now. He had no idea what had happened at the Lanning house today, but the Lannings wanted Linyah to come back there too. "Well?"

Nic looked at his sister and dad. Dad wasn't so much pissed as he was amused; it was written in every part of his face. It was his sister that was pissed. And whenever she looked at his dad, he tried his best to look upset as well. Nic didn't think he was fooling anyone. His mom walked into the room just as Nic was going to explain again that he had no idea where Linyah had gone.

"You should know that sending him out to find her would be a fool's errand. If she doesn't want us to find her, we never shall. We are leaving in the morning and she's nowhere to be found, and I think that it would be foolish to go about this halfcocked. I want her here now as well, but we have no knowledge as to what might have happened to her in that household."

Nic looked at the room and wondered if maybe she was there and hiding under the piles of clothing that were everywhere. She might be in here and no one could see her. But he looked at his mom again and knew that she'd looked. And well.

"What happened today, Nic?"

"I'm not sure. Phillip said she was there for a while and that his dad had hurt his mom. Linyah had stepped in, but that Thomas had come home and found them. I don't know what happened, other than there is some confusion as to whether or not she's his female." His mom sat down and his dad stood up. Kendra only sat there looking like the queen she was, but Nic knew her best. She was upset. And he wasn't really sure why just yet.

"You mean that man who hurt his wife is a male to my daughter?" Nic shook his head and started to explain, but his dad was on a roll. "I should hope not. We will not have a threesome living here like that. Who is this male she is supposed to be with? That young Phillip person?"

"No. Another brother by the name of Thomas. I've never met him, but I guess he was there when Linyah was. He kissed her." His mother made an odd noise, but Nic didn't think she sounded unhappy. "I'm not sure what's going on. It just might be a mistake or something."

"Not if she's run off, you can bet it's not." His dad thundered around the room for several minutes before he turned to him again. "She's gone to the mountains, hasn't she?"

"I would say that's a good bet." He even knew where she might be in the mountains but didn't tell his dad. If she needed to be there, then she had a good reason. "She has a great many hidey holes up there, and it would be years if not decades to find her if she doesn't want to be found."

"But you will." He wanted to tell him no, but his father nodded. "You will. Bring that young man here too. I want to meet him and see his worth. Not that I don't think Linyah can handle him if he's anything like his father, but I should meet the man who would take my daughter. Do you think he'd live here?"

"I want you to bring Linyah here first." Everyone looked at Kendra. "I want to have a word with her before we bring a man here. It would be better for...I want to have a word with her."

"And what do we do if this man, this Thomas person, is not worth our time?" His dad shook his head. "No. Bring them here. Both of them. Now." It wasn't often that his dad overrode what Kendra said, but he did this time. And Kendra only nodded. But she did leave them then. No one said a word to her as the door closed behind her. His dad told him to go and find Linyah and this man.

"I don't know, Dad. But to bring him here, don't you think that would upset her more?" His dad nodded and smiled. "I see. So what do you want me to do? Kidnap him and toss him in a cell with her?"

"Sound plan. I like it." His dad patted him on the back, and Nic tried to tell him he was kidding, but he wasn't hearing him. "Go get him, find your sister, and tie them together if you have to. I want them together. I can meet him later, I suppose, but it's important that we keep them together. If we don't, then well, she'll never come here again. Well? Go and get him."

Nic hated it, but he left the castle for the Lannings. The leap was gathered in a large house that he immediately thought of Linyah living in. He didn't even know who the house belonged to, but loved it for his sister. Misha stood up when he entered the room they were gathered in.

"I'm to take Thomas to my home to help me find my sister." The man who he thought was Thomas stood up, then sat down. "You are the man who would claim her? The man who kissed her today?"

"I should just let her run, but I'm being forced into this by my family." Thomas glared at Misha before looking at him again. "I don't want a mate, but she's mine and I'd have her here as soon as possible."

"You will be well equipped to know that she doesn't want you either. In fact, I would like to suggest that you leave her where she is and you'll live longer." Thomas stood up and started pacing. Nic wanted to laugh. They were not even together and he could see that they had a great deal in common. "You will come with me to find her?"

"Yes." Thomas looked at his family, then back at him. "I really don't have a choice in the matter. She and I have...I kissed her, and all I can think about is having more of her."

Nic was surprised at the surge of anger that came over him. But the big leopard seemed to understand. When Thomas put out his hand to him, Nic took it and felt the connection almost immediately. His sister was going to be in good hands. Provided that she didn't kill him first.

He moved them through space to his sister's room. He was surprised to see his parents still there. His dad stood up, and Thomas bowed before him. He wanted this to be right and decided that starting off on the right foot was better than the wrong one any day. Thomas apparently thought so as well.

"Thomas Lanning, I'd like to present to you my parents. This is my father, Lord Nildale, of the Genjar people. He is lord to most of the upper lands that surround this realm." He took him to his mother, who had not risen but sat like the queen she used to be. Thomas took her hand when she offered it to him and kissed it on the back. "This is my mother, Second Queen of the Genjar people, Retired Queen of the Sixth Order of Genjar, Queen Sina."

"You're a leopard. A half-breed but a good man." Thomas smiled at his mother. "I'm too old to beat around the bush, young man. When I have something to say, I say it. I do hope you can live with that. My daughter is ten times worse than me."

"I've not had the pleasure of speaking to her as yet." He smiled again when he looked around the room. "Did she do this in a fit of rage?"

"No. I'm afraid she's a mess. And this is not nearly as bad as it normally is." Thomas paled and looked at Nic to see if he was kidding, he was sure. "You don't like clutter, I take it."

"No. I have a place for everything and everything…she lives like this? All the time?" Nic wanted to laugh but just held on. If this was disturbing to the young leopard, he'd hate for him to see her office. It was worse than this. "All the time?"

"I'm afraid she does." His father answered Thomas as if he were proud of the mess. "She can find anything in a moment too. I've seen her mother look for something in her office for an hour and she'd go right in, pick it up, and hand it to her. Just like she knew where it was all the time. Well, I suppose she did. She has her own system, she said."

"She's a mess. I can't stand a mess." Thomas looked at him pleadingly. "Please tell me this is not her room. And that I'll find her to be as neat and orderly as I am. Please? I beg of you."

"I'm afraid that I'm messier than this." Everyone turned at the sound of Linyah's voice. "If I were you, I'd run now before I got any of my dirtiness on you."

"You can't possibly be this callous about your things. Surely you want to keep things nicer than this?"

She looked around the room and Nic could almost see her mind weighing her options. She was going to have this man running for cover before anyone could do anything about it.

"Yeah, I am. And you know what else? You should see my bathroom. I leave hair in the tub and toothpaste on the sink. It's sort of my tribute to art I think. I have some very interesting forms in there. Would you like to see them?" Nic started to go between the two of them when his dad stopped him. He wasn't sure what Thomas was planning, but he was bent on doing it. He and his parents were out of the room just as Linyah screamed. Nic was going back in when his father laughed.

"She's in good hands. I think this is a match made in heaven." Nic started to tell him he was nuts when he laughed again. "Yes, sir, that boy is going to have his hands full, but I think that Linyah is going to be the loser this time. He looks like he can whip her into shape. Be nice, won't it? To have her all shipshape? Of course, she will give him his due too, I suppose. Yes, sir, a match made in heaven."

His parents moved down the hall laughing. Nic stood outside the room for several minutes, not hearing a thing and worrying. When his dad said his name, he turned to see him standing a few feet away. He was frowning now, and Nic didn't know what to do with all this.

"Come away, son. She doesn't need you rescuing her. Not with this man. He will not harm her." He asked how he knew she wouldn't hurt him. "Because she can't. They are now a couple whether they want it or not."

Nic had a feeling that neither of them was going to survive this. And he wasn't sure who to root for to come out on top. He loved his sister, but this man, Thomas Lanning, was a good man too, one that he thought he could really like. He just hoped that he lived long enough to get to know him. Smiling, he followed his parents down the hall. Linyah didn't need him. And he was happy for whatever the two of them worked out.

~~~

Thomas picked her up by putting his shoulder into her belly and tossing her on the bed. When she scrambled away from him, he grabbed her ankle and held her. That's when he saw the blood pouring from a wound on her chest. Before she could get away from him again, he told her to stop. She stilled immediately.

"What happened here?" He fought with her but in the end got her shirt up. The padding was saturated with blood, and he gently peeled it away. "Christ. What happened?"

"I wasn't paying attention when we were after the rogue." She tried to pull the shirt back down, but he ripped it from her. "You're paying for that."

"Bill me." He ran his finger over the blood and then watched her face as he took it to his mouth. When he moaned, he felt her body react to him and he had to fight hard to not pull her to him and taste more than just her blood, actually more of all of her. The thought of burying his mouth over her sex had him aching to strip her down completely. He had to take a deep breath, which really didn't help before he could speak again. "How come you're not healing?"

She didn't look like she was going to answer but when she did, he could see that she was in more pain than he'd first thought. "I can't heal myself. It's forbidden. And now because you have to be a big man, I'm hurting again. Why don't you go back to where you came from and leave me the hell alone? I don't want a male to think he's going to rule me."

"I don't want a female at all. And I would never presume to rule anyone." He helped her sit up and then pulled the rest of the padding away. There were more wounds on her back, and someone had done a pissy job of stitching them up. "Who is your surgeon? Whoever he is, he needs to be fired."

"*She* stitched me up as best she could." Thomas turned her around after helping her stand up. Her back was not as bad as her front, but he did want to help her. Leaning in, he could smell the infection, and his cat snarled at him. Linyah turned and looked at him; that was when he knew she had felt his other self as well. He tried to smile at her, but he wanted her, both of them did.

"He wants to help you. So do I." Linyah pulled away, but he brought her back to his body so that her back was to his chest, and even as gentle as he tried to be, he knew that he'd hurt her again. "Please stand still and let me fix this. These stitches in your back have been...I think they didn't clean the wound well and you're getting sicker."

"She cleaned them. I heard her saying she was." But there was doubt there, he could hear it. "What can you do? I'm not...you're right, I should have been better by now. When I was in my cave, I ran hot, then cold. I never do that. I came back to have her look at the wounds again. Something just isn't right."

"I'm going to have you lay down and I'm going to tear the stitches out. But I need help. I'd like to take you to my house and have my mom help us. She used to be a nurse and she'd know what to do." Her nodding had him pulling her tighter. "I can't get us to my house if I don't know where we are."

In seconds he was standing in his kitchen. Reaching for his mother, he felt that Linyah had gone limp in his arms. Fear made him reach for both Misha and Phillip. Phillip said he'd get her family and Misha was on his way. He took her to his room and laid her on his bed. As soon as she was naked, he could see her body was riddled with tears in her skin. Most of them were scars, but a few, mostly on her chest and back, were black and blue. She looked as if she'd been dragged behind something and then left alone. Thomas felt his cat tear at him to maim whoever had hurt what was his.

"Mother fuck." He turned to look at her brother, who had just come into the room. He looked as if he'd seen a ghost, and Thomas pulled a sheet up and over her body. It was saturated almost as soon as it touched her body. "She didn't tell me she was still hurting. Not once. I had no...he attacked when we were apart. She said he'd only gotten her back. And when I saw these a few days ago, they didn't look this bad. I had...she's sick."

"My mom is going to help her. But you have to see to the person who did this to her. I don't mean the rogue, but the person who stitched her up. They had to know that they were leaving her to infection." Nic nodded and when he continued to stand there, Thomas shook him. "You have to go now. If this woman is aware that you know what happened, she'll run. Go and get her."

He disappeared just as Thomas was reaching for his mother again to have her please hurry. Her mother and father came into the room just as his mom entered by the door. Thomas had to hold tightly onto his temper when her mother started barking orders at everyone, including him. Finally, it was Hannah who took control as soon as she entered the room. Misha just stood back and let her take charge.

"Sit down and shut the fuck up. I don't know what planet you're from, but here we do not tell a man what to do in his own home." Linyah's father stood up, and Misha moved to stand behind Hannah. As soon as he sat back down, Hannah spoke again. "Now. We're going to be calm and cool here. If you think you can add something to help, then we'll listen. Otherwise, it might go faster if you let us take care of what we need to do. These men are professionals and they can do things you can only dream of. Now. What the hell happened to her?"

"She was out bringing in a rogue. And so you know, I'd very much like to hit you but I'm fearful you'll hit me back. But I must say, I'm impressed, young lady. My daughter and you will get along well, I think." Hannah thanked Sina. "She and Nic had gone after one of our own. A rogue. I never heard the entire thing, only that he'd managed to hurt her and nearly got away. We had no idea that the damage was this extensive. I was informed that other than a few scratches she was going to be fine."

"The doctor stitched the wounds closed without cleaning them out." His mom handed a small slither of something to Sina. "I just took that out of the first wound we opened. I'm afraid that you'll all need to leave so that I can take care of the rest of them. I can't think when there are this many people arguing. Hannah will see to you as well as that nice cook, Mike."

"I'll help you." Sina stood up and rolled up her sleeves. "I used to doctor my own troops when they fell on the battle ground. My daughter…Kendra is our older daughter…I just heard from her, and she is making sure that the doctor is taken care of. But I'd very much like to stay and help in any way that I can."

Thomas wasn't sure his mom was going to let her, but her short nod had him letting out a breath he'd not realized he'd been holding. As soon as the rest of the occupants were out, his mom ordered him to get clean rags, water, and for him to shift. He had Mike get what they needed, and he stripped down and shifted in the bathroom. Thomas had a long talk with himself before going back to the bedroom. His cat seemed pleased with the turn of events; Thomas wanted to strangle him.

She's your mate, you moron. Get a grip. So what if she's a slob? You can pick up after her. He nodded to his reflection in the mirror. *Even if you have to hire a person to follow her around, she's your mate and she needs you to help her.*

Moving down off the counter, he moved into the bedroom to find her mother holding her down while his was pulling stitches out. Linyah wasn't screaming, but her moans of pain tore through him. As he leapt up on the bed, Sina stared at him. She didn't look terrified, but she did look extremely uncomfortable.

"He won't hurt you." Sina nodded at his mom without taking her eyes from him. "He can calm her maybe. Back away a little and see if she'll accept him. It might go easier for her if he can get her to calm down."

Thomas moved closer to Linyah's hot body. She was burning up with fever and his cat wanted to lick the wounds closed for her. But his mom cautioned him to wait until they were cleaned. As soon as he was snuggled near her, her arm wrapped around him and she pulled him to her. He looked at his mom when she nodded.

"It'll go better now, I think." Thomas hoped so. His cat wanted revenge for what had happened to his mate, and Thomas wanted to exact his own sort of punishment. As they worked on her, he felt Misha touch his mind.

Nic has put the doctor in a cell. She was leaving town when she found out that Linyah had fallen ill so quickly. Thomas asked him what that meant. *She thought it would be a good deal longer before the infection took its toll on her. She was under the impression that if Linyah fell ill, then her brother, the rogue they captured, would be set free. The doctor didn't care so much for her brother being the target of a manhunt when there were other people still running around. She thinks it was him being chased by the authorities that made him go wrong. Nic told her, and not at all nicely, that they wouldn't have been chasing his ass had he not killed anyone in the first place. Idiot. How is your mate?*

She's a slob. Misha laughed. *I kid you not. Her room looked like she'd torn everything out of the closet, then tossed it about the room during a windstorm. I had to...Christ, she's my mate.*

That she is. And a hell of a one too. Her brother said that she's been working as a hunter for a great many years. By the way, you're much younger than her. By thousands of years. Apparently, and this is from her father, Genjar royalty live forever unless they have their head removed. It's apparently the only way to kill them. I had to go and look up about their race. They'd been considered long gone for longer than most people have been alive. Her fingers tightened in Thomas's fur and he moved closer to her as Misha continued. *Thomas, we have to go on a mission. I don't think you should go with us this time. We might be gone a while.*

I can't leave her. Misha said he understood more than he could say. *I'll catch up if she gets better, but right now, I can't leave her.*

You do what you have to do. I know that this is much more important. I'd stay too, but this one...there are children involved. And Hannah is breeding. Thomas asked him if she knew. *Not yet. I didn't want to freak her out. She's terrified of being a parent. I didn't even realize she was in heat until it was too late. And all she has talked about for weeks now is that she might go and get fixed. I had to ask her what "fixed" meant. You don't think she's serious, do you? Anyway....*

Misha told him where they were headed and that he'd appreciate hearing from him about his mate. He even asked him if he'd keep an eye on Hannah as well. She was worried about her grandparents showing up. Thomas told him he'd take care of it.

His bed had to be stripped down and changed when they were finished cleaning her up. One of his shirts, something soft and clean, was put on her when they declared they'd gotten the infection out as best they could. While his mom and Sina cleaned up, he held Linyah in his arms after shifting back and pulling on a pair of soft pants. His mom asked him if he needed help giving her a quick shower.

"She's soaked through with blood and sweat. And her hair is matted. She might feel better; I know I would." Thomas said he'd do it, and soon after they left him. He was holding her, trying to figure out what to do about a shower, when he realized something. He'd never taken a shower with a woman before, much less one that was unconscious.

Laying her on the bed, he decided that he'd get everything ready before he took her in. As the room warmed up, he pulled out towels, another one of his shirts, as well as some of his old socks. Going back in to get her, he decided to stay dressed so if she did wake up, he'd not piss her off too much. And he was reasonably sure that finding them both naked in the shower would do just that. It was time to do what he could to make her feel better.

Lifting her up, he took her into the large shower. He was glad now that he'd had this place renovated first and all the rooms enlarged. He was trying to figure out how to wash her hair when she opened her eyes. He didn't move as she looked at him.

"You're going to be better now." She nodded but still hadn't moved. "My mom said you'd feel better if you were cleaned up. I was trying to figure out how to wash your hair without getting soap in your eyes."

He was babbling. Thomas wanted to stand up and let her finish her bath by herself, but he was reluctant to let her go. Instead, he pulled her to his chest and sat her on his lap on the smallish seat that had been installed when the shower had been replaced. While holding one arm around her waist, he finished with her hair and even got it rinsed out before she leaned back to him.

"I feel like I've been beaten up and left for dead." Thomas simply held her, not sure what he should do now. He wanted her, there was no doubt of that, but he knew that she was too weak to try to do much more than she was right now. "I was hurting so badly. That's why I came back when you were in my room. I was going to see the doctor again. She did this to me, didn't she?"

"Yes. She stitched your wounds closed without cleaning them properly. She's been arrested. Her plan was to make you very ill so that her brother, the man you and Nic had captured, could be freed." Linyah nodded and when she did, her breast brushed against his hand. "You should try to stand up. I'm not...I can't hold you this way for much longer."

"You want me." For an answer he moved her wet hair from her shoulder and kissed her shoulder before moving down to her spine. Her moan had him nipping at her again and again until he knew that he was going to take her if they continued. "I've never had sex before. I mean, I say I have because who gets this old without experimenting it at least once or twice, right? But it never interested me before. I'd very much like to have sex with you. Today. Now."

"I'm glad to know that it interests you now. Because I have to tell you, it interests me a great deal. Christ, I hope so." His cock was so hard it was painful. Adjusting her so that he could reach his cock and adjust himself, she lifted his hand to her breast and he cupped her tightly in his hand. "We're not in any position to have sex right now."

"Why not?" Why not indeed, his mind screamed at him. "I mean, I'm naked, you're nearly so. And very hard. Are you as hard and thick as you feel right now?"

She moved on his lap, and he had to still her with his hand at her hip. But touching her warm, wet skin only made him want more, and he slid his hand to between her thighs. Christ, she was hot. He slid his fingers just over her curls and wanted to dig into her just this one time. But he knew, as surely as he was sitting there, that there would never be just this one time.

"I'm not going to make love to you while you're still hurting." He stood up, pressed her against the shower wall, and rocked into her ass. "Do you have any idea how badly I want you? How much I want to drink from your pussy until you come down my throat? I want to fuck you. I want to bend you over this seat and slam my cock as deep into you as I can go."

"Make me come, Thomas. Please?" He rocked again and then slid his fingers into her heat. He'd been wrong, she wasn't hot. She was fucking molten. "Please. I need this. Help me."

Thomas could feel the sweat bead on his back. Even with the hot water slushing down over him, he was still sweating, and kicked off his pants. Touching his finger to her hard nubbin, he spread her legs wider as she rocked into his touch. As badly as he wanted to bury himself deep inside of her, he wanted her to come for him even more. Pinching her clit again, he tugged at her nipple and bit into her flesh at her shoulder when she cried out. His cock, full and aching, released all over her as she cried out again and again. He knew the mistake he'd made, but could find no reason right then to regret it. Christ, he wanted more. But what he'd done had sealed the deal for them.

Thomas had just marked his mate.

CHAPTER 4

Linyah wasn't sure how she felt about her male. He was quiet and she could tell that he was upset about something, but instead of just telling her what was going on, he simply moved about the room as if he had the weight of the world on his shoulders. Finally she told him to sit down. He only stood there looking at her for a long time.

"You're very bossy. Has anyone ever told you that before?" He didn't sit down but continued to move about the room, driving her insane. "And I don't take well to orders. You want me to do something, then you ask. Politely. I'm not any more an animal than you are. Not right now, at any rate."

"You won't do it anyway, so I might as well get something out of this. I want to know what happened." He cocked a brow at her, and she felt her face heat up. "I mean with Zin, the surgeon. She said that she healed me. Why did she change her mind? She had to know that her brother was going to die for his actions. Why on earth did she think that me being sick would make anyone set him free? I just don't understand how her mind was working in this. If it was at all."

"I don't know what she said to your brother, but he told me what I told you. And I agree. There had to be more than her just wanting him released. And to keep you from healing makes no sense either. Nic said she refuses to talk until she's released. Will that happen, you think?"

Linyah shook her head. Her sister didn't like her, but there was no way she'd let a criminal go.

"Did you know that you're going to have to behead her? I mean, be the one that carries out the sentence?"

"Yes. It's a part of my job as head of security. But I'm not going to have to do this one. Nic said he'd take care of it for me." She was distracted and didn't notice right away that he'd stopped moving and was staring at her. "What is it now?"

"You're not even going to have a trial for her? See what you could have done to make it so she didn't try to kill someone else?" She wanted to point out that if she were dead, she wouldn't be hurting someone else, but he continued. "Is this how your kind deals with people? You simply kill them without benefit of them saying why they did it?"

"She tried to kill me. I think that in and of itself is enough to have her beheaded, don't you? Or do you wish now she'd finished the job?" He was on top of her in a heartbeat. As he moved down her body, he pulled the shirt, which he'd tossed at her when they came out of the bathroom, from her shoulder. The place where he'd bitten her was hot and she wanted to beg him to bite her again. "What are you doing?"

"Do you think I like the fact that you were nearly killed by this woman and there is nothing I can do about it? I nearly lost you today. What would have happened to us if...?" He lifted his head and she could see that he was taking in her scent. His next words, spoken harshly and deep, made her entire being tighten and expand. "I love the scent you give off. The way you smell when you're aroused. Would you like to come again? This time filling my mouth with your juices? Then when I've had my fill of drinking from you, you'd let me slide deep inside of you until your pussy was wrapped tightly around me?"

"Please?" She felt breathless, needy, and hot. When he took her nipple into his mouth through her shirt, it was all she could do not to beg him again to take her. But he lifted his head and looked down at her, and she suddenly felt afraid of him. When he moved back, she wanted to stomp her foot and demand that he take her. This running hot and cold shit was going to drive her nuts.

"I'm going to wait until you're healthy. But until then, I want you so close to the edge that you beg me to take you." When she sat up, she could see his cock pressed hard against his pants front, and she wanted to touch him. But he cupped his cock in his hand and took a few more steps back. "You have to be healthy when I take you."

"Why?" She watched him. He was fighting with himself, she could see that. He turned around, walked to the fireplace, and leaned heavily against it. Linyah felt like getting up and hitting him.

"I'm not going to hurt you while I take you. And believe me, when I take you, I want you fully aware that I'm doing so." She felt her body respond to his words, and he looked at her. Spreading her legs wider, she watched his nostrils flare again and his body stiffen. "You're playing with fire, Linyah. I'm not a soft man who likes soft sex. I like it hard, painfully so, and I want you to scream when you come for me."

"Come here." He moved to face her but didn't come toward her. He stared intently at her and she knew that she had him. "Come here and show me what you want. I have no idea why I want you to take me right now. My need for you is so incredible that all I can think of is you pounding deep inside of me until I can't tell you from me."

"Show me." Standing up, she pulled off her shirt and let it fall to the floor. She was completely naked now. He moved toward her in a slow, almost cat-like motion then. She supposed that was just what he was doing, as she could see his cat as he raced over his skin. "He wants to mark you as well. Taste your pussy too. Would you let him? Let him drink from you until you come for him?"

"Yes." He pulled off his tee-shirt and dropped it on the floor. As he pulled his pants off, standing not five feet from her, Linyah felt her body heat more for him. The things she thought he was going to do to her made her want to hold onto something so that when he did touch her she wouldn't fly away. "What do you need me to do?"

"Don't run." He shifted just like that, his body going from male to cat all in one smooth movement. She reached for the bedpost and held on as he made his way to her. When he nudged his nose against her flesh, she ran her fingers through his soft fur.

He pushed her onto the bed with his big head. Then he moved to sit between her thighs, and she felt her juices flow. He was going to touch her there, taste her, and she held her breath when he moved toward her. As soon as his nose touched her she came, crying out his name as he licked her over and over. Every time he made her come, every time that he drank more from her, she wanted more of him. When he lifted his head from her, she watched as the cat disappeared. Then Thomas was kneeling between her legs.

He wasted no time in burying his face at her pussy. While the cat's tongue had been rough and long, his was smooth and talented. Curling his tongue deep within her set her off again, and she begged him to take her. But he ate at her, licked her, and suckled her clit into his mouth until she was weak from coming. Then he stood up, fisting his cock as he stared down at her.

"I'm not going to be gentle." She nodded and reached for him. Linyah had no idea, but she thought that he'd tell her no, but he wrapped his hand around hers as she touched him and watched her. "If I come on you now, I'll be able to take you slowly. I don't want to hurt you. Well, I do, but not this time."

"Why not?" The pearl of white cum leaked from the tip of him, and she licked it from his cock. He moaned and she leaned in to take more. Taking his crown into her mouth, she curled her tongue around him and tasted all of him. When he pulled her head up, she looked at him.

"I'm going to come this way if you keep that up." She nodded and took him into her mouth again. "Christ, you're making me see stars. I want to fuck you, fuck that pretty mouth of yours."

He rocked into her mouth, and for the first few strokes she had to figure out how not to gag. But when she swallowed, he cried out and told her again. She needed something too, and slid her hand down her body to touch her where he had. But he pulled from her mouth and told her to lay back.

His cock was glistening with her saliva, and she wanted to take him again, knowing that if she did this time, he'd fill her mouth with all of him. But he moved onto the bed with her, and she knew he was going to fuck her. When he laid over her, his cock at her entrance, she stiffened, not sure now that he was there.

"Don't, baby. I need to be inside of you." She nodded but her body was so stiff feeling that she nearly jumped off the bed when he took her nipple into his mouth. "Your nipple reminds me of hard berries. And as sweet too. I wonder if I put a clamp on them, would you come with the feeling or would you cry out when I touched you? And I want to explore you. I want to tie you to this bed and take you anyway I want you."

He suckled just on the tip of her breast until she felt her body loosen. He moved his way down her body, nipping and licking the tiny wound, and she nearly cried out when he licked her pussy again. Thomas said her name, and she looked up at him. He was smiling.

"I'm going to eat you again. Then when you come, I'm going to enter you hard and feel you come around me again and again. I'm going to fuck you, having your ankles wrapped around me while I pound your pretty pussy over and over until you scream out your release. Then I'm going to fill you with my seed, bite you hard, and mark you." She nodded, licking her lips, thinking she'd like to taste him too. "Will you bite me, Linyah? Mark me too?"

"Yes." He buried his face between her legs and brought her to a quick hard climax. When his fingers slid inside of her, she rode him hard as he brought her to two more quick climaxes. As he moved up her body, this time she was ready for him, ready for his cock to take her. When he was at her pussy, his cock sliding in and out of her just enough to want her to beg him for more, he took her mouth as he slammed forward.

Her breath caught. Her body screamed at her to get him off her. She hurt, it was too much. Moving her hips to try and buck him off, she realized he was talking to her. Softly, in her head, he was telling her how sorry he was, how badly he felt for hurting her. When she moved her head to look at him, he wiped at a tear that was on her cheek.

"I'm sorry." She nodded and he moved slowly. The slide of his cock made her moan, and she looked at him. "If you're a really good girl, I'm going to try and not come in you before you come. The way you're gripping me right now, I'll be surprised if I can hold off long enough for you to come at all."

"I need to come." He nodded and moved again. "Please, more."

He was gentle with her, moving in and out of her so slowly that it was hard to imagine him hurting her before. As she lifted her legs up and over his, he shifted his body so that he cupped her ass and brought her harder against him. Linyah cried out her first release of what she was sure would be many more as he moved deeper within her and just a little harder.

Come for me. His command echoed through her head as he started moving faster, his cock not just filling her but becoming a part of her. Even as she felt herself build up again, he was licking his tongue over her shoulder to her throat, and she knew that when she came, he was going to bite her hard enough to draw blood. As soon as the thought of biting him popped into her head, she screamed out, her release taking her hard. His teeth tore into her skin and she did the same to him, tearing deeply until the taste of his blood was all she could think of. As she came again, screaming around his wound, he threw back his head and roared out his release. Linyah felt the world around her tilt just enough that she had to hold onto Thomas or fall.

Even as he dropped onto her, she knew that he was being careful. When he rolled to his back, taking her body with him, she felt his concern that he'd hurt her. Linyah had always been the powerful one in her family, never wanting anyone to cuddle her or hold her so tenderly. But she found that she liked him touching her. Loved him cradling her into his chest and arms.

Linyah yawned once and felt her body start to float. She'd never felt this relaxed before and felt herself drifting off. He moved again, this time bringing a blanket over them, and she smiled. She might get used to having a male if it was like this all the time.

~~~

Hannah threw up again and tried to keep from being too loud at it. The last time she'd been sick, her mo…Bella had beaten her pretty badly for it. Not that she expected anyone to beat her here, but old habits were hard to break. She heard someone in the room next to her and stood up and wiped at her mouth. She came out to find Sina standing in the kitchen, making something at the stove. The thought of food nearly made Hannah go back to the bathroom

"I hope you don't mind, but I don't get tea often; my male hates it, and I thought you could use a cup." Hannah nodded and sat down as Sina continued. "You could eat some crackers; that might help."

"I think I'm coming down with something." Sina turned to look at her, then smiled. "I guess you don't get sick all that often."

"Rarely, as it so happens. And it's been a while since I was sick like you are." Hannah took the cup of tea and felt her belly relax by just the smell. Humming gently, she sipped it and then looked at Sina when she sat. "You're breeding, did you know that?"

Hannah didn't know what she meant and it took her several seconds before she got it. Putting her hand on her belly, she stood up and then sat down. She was going to kill Misha. Sina smiled at her again. But then maybe he didn't know either.

"He does know. I'm sure he's known all along but didn't want to upset you. You are upset, aren't you?" She nodded. "I can tell. You'll be a wonderful mother. I know...I've looked into your mind. I hadn't meant to go that deeply, but I could tell that you'd been hurt. I was worried...well, I was worried about my daughter staying here with men who might be abusive. So I looked. I'm glad to know that it wasn't Misha."

"I would never harm her. None of us would. I really like your daughter. She's a lot like I wish I was." She sipped the tea. "This is amazing. What is it?"

"A brew of mine. Like I said, my male hates the smell. I have no idea why, but he does. While I try to give him whatever he wants, this is something that I missed. I shall leave you some for your tummy." Hannah nodded. Maribel came in just as Sina was making them another cup, and she joined them.

"I'm going to have a baby." Maribel laughed. "I guess you knew too. How come I'm the last to know? And he's going to pay for this when he gets back."

"I'm sure he will. Now I can give you those things I've been hiding away for you." She left them alone, only to return a few minutes later with bags and bags of things.

Hannah was so overwhelmed by it she started to cry. These people were just too kind to her.

"Nonsense." Hannah looked up at the woman standing in the doorway. "You are getting just what you need from them and they're happy to give it to you. I don't think we've met before. I'm Linyah, daughter of Sina and Nildale, sister to Nic and Kendra."

"I'm Hannah Lanning. This is my mother-in-law, Maribel Lanning. You know my husband, Misha." Linyah sat down but stood up again when her mother started to rise. She fixed her a cup of tea and then gave her a glass of water.

"Tea is good for your belly, but you need to drink more. You're dehydrated and you need more meat. Red meat." Hannah nodded and looked at the other two women with her. "They'll agree with me too. We can all tell that you are a little on the undernourished side and need much more liquid."

"Thank you, but it's that...I don't...I'm not used to people being nice to me." Linyah nodded but said nothing. "You've read my mind as well. I don't think I like you guys doing that."

"Would you like to do it too?" Hannah started to shake her head no, but Linyah continued. "It's something I can share with you. You won't be able to read mine because I gave you the ability, but you can read anyone else's. My mother included." There was a hint of anger there but Hannah let it pass.

Instead of answering her right off, she changed the subject. "Do you know what I'm going to have?" Linyah put her hand on her belly, and Hannah felt a strange kind of connection with her. When she pulled her hand back, she smiled. "Do I want to know what you found out?"

"It's a boy. He's like his father but more. I would say that instead of being only about fifty-percent leopard, he's more like seventy-percent. Do you want to know when he'll be born?" Hannah shook her head. "Okay. But if you change your mind, let me know."

"How can you do that?" Maribel stood up and so did Sina, as if on cue. She wondered if she'd offended them, but Linyah asked her to stay seated when Hannah rose from her seat as well. As soon as they were alone, she looked around the room.

"I've asked to speak to you alone. My mother knows, but Maribel doesn't know that I'm having a sort of hard time here. I don't know what I'm doing and was wondering if you could help me." Hannah was so confused she was sure it was written all over her face. "I have never had a male that touches me like Thomas does and wants to...he wants things from me that I don't know how to give him."

Hannah knew that Misha had called to speak to Thomas that morning. Then Thomas left in a hurry. Apparently the search they were on wasn't going well and they had called him in. Even Nic and his dad had gone to help. It was the worst rescue they'd been on in a while. And they needed all the extra people they could get. Hannah wondered why they'd not asked Linyah to go, then remembered that she'd been hurt.

"You know what kind of upbringing I had, I take it?" Linyah nodded and Hannah continued. "I was so overwhelmed by this family that it took me until recently to get used to the fact that they love to touch and be touched. The only way the woman who raised me touched me was with a hard object and her fists. And if not hers, then someone else's. I didn't come from this sort of family. So I can relate to how strange it is to you."

"You certainly took on my mom." Hannah flushed. "She told me about it. She said you put her in her place and then were so kind to her she couldn't help but like you. I guess she thinks you and I will get along well too. Me being bossy and all." Hannah didn't know about all that. She liked the woman a great deal so far. Hannah thought that if she got some answers from Linyah, she'd have a better understanding on how to answer her.

"What kind of things does Thomas want from you?" Linyah got up and fixed her another cup of tea and refilled her empty water glass. Hannah sipped it before continuing. It really was making her feel better. "I mean, if you don't want to share, I understand."

"It's not that. I'm not really sure what I mean, to be honest. But nobody just gives things like he did without wanting something in return." Hannah asked her what it was and she put a key on the table. "I don't understand why he'd give me a key to his house. Then when I asked him what he wanted of mine, he said nothing I wasn't willing to give. What does that mean?"

"It means he trusts you." Linyah looked as confused as she felt most of the time. "Look, what do you have that means the very world to you? Something that no one else in the world has ever touched, seen, or maybe even knew was yours."

"My swords. I have a collection of them I've been saving for decades. No one…well, maybe Nic knows, but he doesn't know how many. They're mine and I don't think anyone would understand why I have them. I don't even use them."

Hannah got up and pulled a large tin from behind the cereal she loved. She dumped the contents on the table and looked at it when Linyah did. It was just over ninety dollars in cash and change, money she'd had when she lived with Bella.

"It was all I had in the world. And it was something that I earned. Whenever I feel overwhelmed by all this...," she waved her hand around the gigantic room, "I pull this out and count it out. It's mine. No one gave it to me, but I earned it. I don't need it. Misha gives me whatever I want, but this is mine. Understand?"

"I do. You treasure it because of what it represented when you lived with that woman. Not what you had but what you rose from. I understand it more than you can know." Hannah smiled and nodded. "Like my swords."

"Yes. And his house; Thomas's house means the same to him. He worked hard to get it ready for himself. Picked out the carpet himself, had the painters come in and help him tear down wallpaper and then paint; it was his. And now, he's sharing it with you. Willingly giving you a piece of his life that no one else has seen. You've been in the house more than we have since he moved in." Hannah hoped she was telling her the right thing and nearly told her that she might be wrong, but she smiled at her and she knew the woman got it.

"He said he wanted me to stay there while he was gone. Told me I could change whatever I wanted. Since I have no idea what to do there, I came here. My mom...I don't want to disappoint him." Hannah laughed. "You think I will?"

"No. I think that no matter what you do, he's going to love you. I know it's hard to imagine someone loving you that much, but he will. And it will be the kind of love you never dreamed of, the kind that lasts forever and ever and makes you feel like you can take on the world and never look back. The kind of love that creates children and shows you there is a way to move on from what has happened before now." Hannah felt tears roll down her cheeks as she looked at Linyah. "It's the kind that saves you from dying alone and lonely."

"I don't love him." Hannah nodded. "I'm not even sure I want to love someone that much. It's very consuming I think. Not that I don't think it's great, but I just don't think I'm the loving sort of person."

"I think you're going to be pleasantly surprised when you wake up one morning and realize that you have loved him nearly all along. The Lanning men don't take love lightly. They're an all or nothing sort of group of men. And when they love you, they love you with all they are." She smiled then. "We are very lucky women, I think. And I'm going to have a baby by one of them."

Hannah and Linyah sat and talked for over two hours. She pulled out baby clothes to look over just as the other two women came in to join them again. Jackson sent them to the living room so he could start dinner, but brought them snacks and tea throughout the afternoon. Hannah had never had a friend before, not a female one, and thought she and Linyah would be good together. They certainly seemed to have a great start to a good friendship.

CHAPTER 5

Thomas pulled the little girl from the mud and laid her gently down on the sheet that had been brought for her. He took care to make sure that her dress was pulled down straight and that the mud, the mire that she'd been buried in, was off her face as best he could. Thomas felt his heart tighten painfully in his chest as he turned back to his work. He'd pulled three children out in the last hour and it was taking its toll on him. When a shadow fell across him, he looked up to see Misha standing there, and took his hand when it was offered to pull him out of the pit.

"There are only four more to find. I think we can take a break." Thomas nodded and let Misha lead him away. He saw that Nic was pulling another child from the dirt and turned his back on him when Misha spoke again. "I need you to tell me this ends someday. I have to tell you, this is the hardest part of what we do for me. The death of a child is horrific, but when it is because of men who were greedy, I want to tear throats out."

Thomas looked around at the disaster they were working. A bus, a charter bus full of grade-school children on a class trip that had been over filled, had slid off the side of a mountain and ended in a ravine several hundred feet below. They'd been on a trip to see the mountain top and the butterflies that were coming out of their cocoons. The charter company had wanted to pocket some of the money that had been paid to them, he'd bet, by using fewer buses than they needed. It was a story that they'd heard time and time again, but it had never been something they'd had to work on. The result had been that when another car, this one taking up too much of the narrow road, had come around a bend in the road, the driver had moved to get out of his way only to tip it over and flip the bus.

"I don't know what to say about this." Misha nodded as if he had expected that answer. "It must be harder on you with Hannah pregnant too. I can't imagine what the parents of these children are going through."

"Me neither. My heart is dying for them." Misha looked away, toward the tree line that had nothing to do with the scene, before speaking again. "She found out. Apparently your mother-in-law told her. I thought she'd be upset with me when she asked me about it, but she said she spent a delightful afternoon getting to know Linyah and wasn't upset any longer. But she wants to make sure I never keep something like that from her again."

Thomas nodded, not really knowing what to say. He had his own set of problems when it came to a mate. "I'm glad she knows. It was hard for me to not say something to her when she asked me about being tired all the time. I felt badly for her but happy for you both. She's terrified, isn't she?"

"She was, maybe still is a little, but I think she'll be great. I think she's more worried about what her grandparents will say or do when or if they arrive before it's born. They're nuts." They both laughed and Misha smiled at him when he continued. "You've bonded and mated, you and Linyah have, right?"

"We have. And no offense, Misha, but I don't want to talk about her right now." Except he did want to talk about her, and he was almost positive that his brother knew it. "She said she wants me to move back to her part of the country with her. I still don't know where that might be other than it's beautiful. I'm not sure I want to leave my family right now, if ever. I just started on the house. I asked her to give me some time and she said she would. I just don't know about this."

"It's her inability to keep things neat, right?" Thomas frowned and nodded once. "I figured as much. She is the security force there. What did you tell her? I mean, I'm assuming this is what has you so quiet. What did you say to her about the way things are going right now?"

"I'm always quiet." Which he was. But it was weighing heavy on his mind that he'd be living away from his family and his work. And now his new nephew. "She doesn't seem to know what to do. I mean with me. And I don't what to do with her either. I don't...she's still a slob. I don't think I can handle that. And then there's the magic stuff she can do. I'm a little freaked out about that, if you want the truth of it. What the hell am I supposed to do with her being so powerful?"

"You could talk to her. And if that fails, set some ground rules or something. I'm sure you'll work it out." Thomas didn't think that was possible. "What else has you all twisted up like an old woman? You've been in contact with her. You know she's fine, right?"

"She is now. And that's something else I don't understand. She said that she'd heal now. And so would I.

And you want to know how I found out? I cut myself shaving this morning and nearly had a heart attack when I healed over. She heard me cursing and that's how I found out about this crap. She told me I'd be healing faster than normal." Thomas pulled out his knife and ran it over his palm. "Just look at this. What the hell am I supposed to make of this?"

Almost as soon as the blade cut into him, his skin was healing over. There was not even a scar. She said that no matter what happened to him from now on, he'd heal almost immediately. Misha whistled, then laughed.

"This is not funny." That, of course, made him laugh all the harder. "Damn it, Misha, I'm living with a being that is old enough to have been around when there was no us. She can do things that I can't even think about right now, and she fucking reads minds. And she's given that ability to Hannah."

That shut him up. Finally. When he sat there for so long, Thomas was sure he was going to be pissed. Then he'd have to knock him on his ass for threatening his mate. But all he did was nod then look up at him.

"Just mine or everyone's?" Thomas growled low and Misha laughed. "I don't know what has you all upset. So what? You're younger than your mate. Big fucking deal. Your mate is a slob. Well boo hoo for you. You have a nice house, have servants waiting on you hand and foot, and you don't get injured. You have life so fucking tough. You want me to knock you on your ass a few times to see if you cannot only heal from a cut but a busted rib or two as well?"

"Fuck off. How am I supposed to provide for her?" It hung there for several seconds before he realized what he'd said. But he knew that was what it was. He couldn't give her anything that she didn't already have or even want. But Misha only laughed before answering him.

"You love her, you moron." Yeah, well that wasn't going to happen overnight to his way of thinking. But Misha stood up when someone seemed to be coming toward them. Thomas was surprised to see not just Linyah but Hannah and Mike, as well as Jackson. They were handing out sandwiches and bottles of water to everyone they passed. When Linyah was near him, he took the sandwich and pulled her to his body. He needed her to touch him back, but she was still holding herself just a little back from him. Thomas didn't know what to make of the slight pain in the area around his heart.

"You were so stressed that we came to see you." He nodded, overwhelmed at how it made him feel to have her there and not completely sure why. "Hannah said you forget to eat when you do these things, so we brought some food. And some help if you need it."

"I think we're about finished here. There were only a few more children to find when Misha and I took a break. You're right though, it's grueling work and very stressful." She nodded and he pulled her just a little tighter to him when he saw his brother holding onto Hannah. He wasn't jealous, he supposed, but the need to be held like that, to love like that, made him want more. "How did you get here?" He nodded when she flushed. "I see. And everyone was okay with that mode of transpiration?"

"Hannah thought it was a hoot, whatever that means. Jackson took it in stride, I suppose, but Mike said he'd be taking the plane back with you guys. He said that if he were meant to transport like that, someone would have provided him with a barf bag. I had to have Hannah explain to me what that meant." They looked around when someone shouted. The last body had been found. "I didn't know this is what you were doing or I would have helped you. It would have been my pleasure to have helped you in any way I could."

"Your dad and brother helped, which we appreciate. But you needed to rest. You needed to heal." She nodded and took the water when he handed it to her. "I'm glad you're here though. I never thought about how much better I'd feel with you around." Thomas felt silly at admitting that to her, and he had no idea why. This having a mate business was difficult to figure out. But she nodded at him too.

"Me too." She looked around again, and he felt her stiffen. Before he could ask her what was going on, someone moved out of the shadows and walked toward them. She pushed him behind her, and he didn't move. He wasn't so macho to think that if she needed to protect him from something or someone that he could do a better job.

"What are you doing here?" The man only stared at Thomas as she asked him again what he wanted and why he was there. Thomas watched him and decided that he didn't care for the other man, especially the way he looked at Linyah.

"You should have stayed away from here, Linyah. There is danger afoot. I have told you time and time again that you are to stay safe for me. I cannot protect what is mine if you are running around without me." The man smiled at him as he continued. "My name is Timmer. I am her male. She will be mine soon, sooner if she would only settle down and tell me the date."

Thomas had to calm his cat the moment the man said Linyah was his. "Yeah, so not going to happen, buddy.

I'm her male and she's my mate." This time he stepped in front of her and for once, she stayed put. "I don't give a rat's ass who you are or what you think to gain by coming here, but I'd have a look around if I were you. You're in my neck of the woods and we don't take kindly to poachers. We protect what is ours."

"As do I. And Linyah is mine. But I do not understand you. Poachers? Why would I care if you like fish? And this term, 'nekked in the wood'? What do you mean?" Misha laughed, as did Hannah; the man, however, looked ready to boil over. "You will not laugh at me. I am a great man. I have been chosen above all others to take her as my mate. You will stop touching her as of now."

"I don't think so. And if you have a problem with that, then you go and get the person who you think promised her to you and bring them before me. I'll settle this right away." Misha stood up as he continued. "As for poaching? That means that you're trespassing on something that belongs to someone else. In this case, his mate. I'm leader here; this leap is mine. As of the moment she accepted him, she was a part of my leap as well. I would suggest that you get the hell out of here before I let him tear you a new ass."

"You cannot talk to me as such." Misha let a little of his cat go, and the man took a step back. "I will return, and when I do, you will need to give her over to me. Then you will see who the poacher is."

When the man disappeared, everyone turned to look at Linyah. Thomas pulled her to him and was surprised when she didn't struggle. He nodded his thanks to Misha, who took Hannah and left them alone. Thomas wanted to ask so many questions, but he had no idea where to start.

"My sister is responsible for this." Thomas looked down at her when she spoke. "I just asked her about Timmer and she said that she'd told him he'd be my male. It had been arranged before I met you. She said that she'd take care to let him know that he was no longer considered my male. She said...she said she was worried about me."

"You spoke to her?" Linyah nodded. "And did she tell you why she'd not told this man that you had a mate now? Or that he was shit out of luck?"

"She has been trying to contact him since she found out about you. I think...she thought if I had a male she'd not have to be concerned with my welfare so much." He could see she was hurt by that and wondered about it. "My sister and I don't really...she hates me. I don't have a clue why, but she does."

For some reason, Thomas doubted that was true. He couldn't really see why anyone would hate her, unless it was for her inability to clean up after herself. He tried not to think of the mess he'd be coming home to and held her tightly. When she settled against his body, he felt his entire wellbeing shift. He felt as if he'd been given a great gift for some reason.

"It's really too bad for him. But he'll have to learn to live with disappointment." She laughed slightly and he smiled. "We have to have someone straighten this out. I can't have him touching you now. My cat, he gets sort of pissy when my mate is touched by another male. Me too."

"I don't understand why either of you would care." He lifted her chin to see her face. There was no way she didn't get this. "I'm not all that special. I'm sort of...awkward, if you want to know the truth. Not all that much to look at, and I know that I'm a pain in the ass."

"Awkward? How do you figure that?" She shrugged and started to pull away. "No, seriously, how did you come to the painfully wrong conclusion that you're awkward in any way?"

"I'm sort of tall. I mean, next to you I'm not, but usually I tower over men. I'm forever getting hurt by one thing or another. I have big boobs and my feet are forever getting tangled up together when I get in a hurry." He watched as she pointed at each thing she thought of as a defect. "And I have a short fuse."

"Don't forget you're sloppy." She glared at him and he laughed. "Okay, first. Tall? Yes, but that's perfect for us. I can sit you on a counter and fuck you easily because you fit so well. Getting hurt? You're in security, you are going to get hurt for the simple reason that you're hanging with bad guys. If you didn't get a bump or bruise once in a while, you'd be letting more get away than you catch. Your boobs, as you call them, are delicious. Your nipples are succulent, and I love the way that they fill my hand when I suckle at them. I love the way they bounce when I take you. The way that your nipples harden so tightly when you're aroused. Then there is the added fact that I love the way they taste, especially when they're dewy from your need. And Linyah, I need you now."

She nodded and he lifted her up. There were a great many people around them, so simply throwing her to the ground and fucking her hard like he wanted wasn't going to work. Before he could tell her they were going to his hotel, they were in his bedroom. He looked down at her face when he realized she'd taken them just where they wanted to be.

"I thought this would be faster than waiting for you to fly home." He nodded and took her mouth. Christ, he wasn't going to make it to the bed, which was only a few feet away. When she moaned, Thomas did the only thing he could think of and took her to the wall right beside him and ripped her clothing from her. If sex was all they had for the rest of their lives, Thomas thought he could live with her mess. He slammed his cock into her even as she cried out she was coming.

~~~

Linyah wandered around the house twice while she tried to think of something to do. The man who cooked for Thomas had made her a really big breakfast, but that had been over an hour ago. She wasn't hungry, but she was bored. Mike came to tell her she had a phone call just when she was contemplating going back to her home.

"It's Hannah. Hannah Lanning." The woman sounded so unsure of herself that Linyah found herself smiling. The two of them had a great deal in common. "I have to go into town today and I was wondering if you'd like to go with me. My aunt—her name is Wanda Little—wants to talk to me about something. Anyway, she wants to have lunch with me too. I don't know why she does, but I couldn't tell her no. She tricked me."

"How did she trick you?" Linyah decided that she'd go to this lunch thing just to protect the young leopard. She wasn't going to let anyone hurt her new friend. "I mean, did she blackmail you?"

"Oh no, nothing like that. She just asked me if I was busy. Then when I said no, she said good, we can have lunch. She might have done that because I've been sort of avoiding her." Before Linyah could ask her why, she continued. "Not really avoiding her so much as...well, I don't know what to say to her. She's my Uncle Daniel's wife, see, and well you know about my family and all. But while she's nice and all, I have a feeling that she's…I think she might be reporting things back to my grandparents. I know that sounds really paranoid and all, but I really don't want to distrust her, although I find myself doing just that." The last came out in a rush, like she was getting it out before she changed her mind.

"You can read her mind, you know." Hannah didn't say anything, and Linyah understood. "Ah, so you've done that. And now you know that's just what she's doing. You should have just told her that she wasn't going to do that any longer and canceled lunch. Unless you want me to go for another reason. What do you want me to do to her? I will. There are any number of things I can do so you don't have to have lunch with her."

Hannah's laughter rang through the phone, and she was sure that Mike heard her. He smiled at her as he sat a glass of something brown in front of her, then a large plate of cookies. The man was going to kill her if he kept this up. While she waited for Hannah to speak again, she bit down into one of the cookies and moaned. Lemon snaps.

"No. Not just yet anyway. But I would like for you to go with me and help me find something to wear that says 'back off, I'm fine.'" A gun at her hip came to mind, but Linyah said nothing as she devoured two more cookies. "Do you know what I mean?"

"Yes. You want something to give you confidence." When Mike started to hand her three more cookies, she growled at him and he laughed. "I'll go with you, but I don't know how much help I can be. Power dressing to me is wearing my uniform with my hair pulled back so tightly my eyes are crossed. And a gun in my hand. I'm pretty sure that won't work. Not for her but with the restaurant that we're going to. I've noticed that humans frown on guns hanging from one's hip." Hannah laughed, as did Linyah. She really liked this young woman.

After they made arrangements for Hannah to come and get her, they hung up. As she sat there eating the last cookie, she looked at Mike. He just smiled at her when she told him she needed help.

"Anything, mistress. You are but to ask and I will do my best to help you." She wondered what he'd say if she asked him to help her be less sloppy, but mentally shook her head. Maybe next time.

"I have clothes." He nodded. "Yeah, I guess you'd know that. Thanks, by the way, for cleaning up after me. I don't usually have someone that is willing to pick up my gun and put it away."

"You have an assortment of them, if you don't mind me saying so." He turned then and handed her the small switchblade she'd been looking for. "I retrieved this from the washer this morning. If I do find such items, where would you like them stashed so you can find them again?"

She had no idea and said that to him. "Maybe I can have a gun safe brought here. I have more than you've seen and sometimes...especially when I'm hurt...I forget to take them out of my suit before I toss them on the floor."

"I shall have Master Thomas send for one. There are a number of things he is still looking to update and purchase for your home, and this will be something to add to the list." She nodded but made a note to herself to get one for herself. There was no reason for him to pay for it.

"I'm having lunch with Hannah. I'm sure you know her." He nodded again. "Good. She wants my help with her aunt. I don't think I like her, the aunt I mean. She's being underhanded and I can't stand dishonest people. But Hannah I do like. This aunt, do you know her?"

"Not really. I have seen her around the main house and with Mr. Daniel. You will like him. But I'm to gather that you are to help her make an impression." Linyah nodded and took the plate of cookies he handed her. She was going to be buzzing in about an hour and wondered if that was such a good idea. "I have a daughter that might be able to help you. She is a fashion designer for a big magazine. I can give her a call. She's in town for a few weeks. And I'm sure that she will be able to help you both out."

He said he'd set it up, and Linyah called Hannah back. Within twenty minutes they were setting up a meeting with Michelle, Mike's daughter, and Hannah sounded excited. Linyah was excited too. She'd never been shopping with another woman before and had never been in a mall. She avoided them as much as she did dresses. It was the same as a death sentence as far as she was concerned.

As they met up at the food court, Hannah hugged her tightly to her. Linyah wasn't sure about all the touchy stuff, but the other woman seemed to enjoy it. As they waited on Michelle, they talked about the aunt.

"She's not mean or anything, just...pushy. You know what I mean? A couple of times when they were over to the house, Daniel, my uncle, asked her to back off. I'm not sure, but.... Okay, I am sure that my grandparents, particularly my grandfather, is making her do this. I wasn't sure how to find out what he might have over her, but she isn't doing this because she's nosy."

"I could check if you want." Hannah nodded, then looked stressed. "I don't mind. I can do it so that she won't know I was in there. And if you don't want to know, I don't have to tell you what it is, just that he does it if you want."

"It's not that. Well, it sort of is, but I'm worried that he'll come here. My grandfather, I mean. So is she. She thinks that if he doesn't get something soon about me, he's going to simply come here and get me." Linyah knew that wasn't going to happen. "I'm terrified that he'll take me. I don't have any idea why that gives me nightmares, but it does. I'm more afraid of him than I ever was of Bella."

"I can understand that, really. It's the fear of the unknown. And he's someone that you don't know. But are you serious about being afraid he'll take you?" Hannah nodded. "You are a leopard, you know? And from what I know, he's just a human. You could kick his ass all the way back to wherever he was hatched. And you want to know something else? Leopard or not, you're a good deal stronger than you think you are. Just tell him to back the fuck off and be done with him."

"He has a lot of money." Linyah asked her if she wanted to be in his will. "No. I mean, sheesh, Misha has more than I can spend, he tells me. I don't need anything. I can make due with little to nothing when it comes to clothing and other things. Not that it stops him from buying me anything I look at twice. Misha tells me to spend more on myself, but having more than a couple of pair of pants and a few shirts is just stupid."

"I have nine uniforms and four pair of boots. This pair of jeans and five shirts that I wear around the house." She looked at her shoes that she'd had longer than she could remember. "I would fall off heels if made to wear them, I don't do dresses, and I hate having my hair touched. I understand you completely, but that makes me no less secure than you when it comes to spending money on myself."

"But you're beautiful." Linyah was shocked by her words and shook her head. "But you are. You have the most beautiful hair I've ever seen. The greenest eyes that...they remind me of emeralds. You're rail thin and well-toned. I bet you work out every day to have a nice, strong body like yours."

"I do run." Hannah nodded. "And speaking of beautiful women, have you looked in the mirror? Christ, woman, you could be on the cover of those girly rags; you know, the magazines that tell you how to improve your sex life? You'd be the most popular cover they'd ever had. If that was something you wanted to do."

Hannah laughed and told her she was nuts. "I see what I look like. I love me as a cat. She's so sleek and beautiful. And her strength amazes me. She can also do things that I can only dream about."

Before she could tell her they were the same person, Michelle came to their table. Mike had provided a picture of her and when she smiled, Linyah could see a bit of her dad in her. She gushed over helping them and took them to a store that looked like something that her sister Kendra would love. As Michelle and Hannah looked at dresses, Linyah wandered around the store. Thomas, who had been called away again, spoke to her.

I might be late getting home tonight. He had left her this morning for the office and said he'd be home by five. It wasn't even ten now, so she asked him if it was a call. *No. We have some paperwork that we have to do and then there is this scheduling thing that Misha is working on. It was my idea, so I'm going to stay and explain it to him so that he can help me with it. It's a chart we're making for our services. I think it might be better if people knew up front how much things were going to cost.*

Okay then. Now she didn't have a clue what to do with the rest of her day. *I'm at the mall with Hannah. She needed some help with a dress. I'm not helping her, but Mike has a daughter that is helping her. Hannah is going to meet with her aunt and needed a boost.*

Are you going to get you a few things? She wanted to be pissy about the question, but his voice had taken on a slight purr sound. *I think there's a shop in the mall that specializes in sexy things. Maybe if you got something to model for me, we might actually make it to the bed this time.*

They had yet to make it anywhere close to the bed when they'd had sex. A few times they'd ended up there afterwards or had used it as a starting point, but they rarely stayed there. Linyah felt her face heat up when she thought about the dining room table that they'd christened just last night.

I don't need anything, but I might take a look. You keep ripping my things from me and I might have to buy in bulk. He laughed. *I have some things at home. Maybe I should just go and bring a few more things here. Just until you figure out what you want me to do.*

What do you mean? I want you to live with me. She nodded and realized he wasn't able to see her and answered him verbally. *You do like living there, don't you?*

I guess. I'm bored out of my mind, but you have a really nice place. She wandered over to the changing room when she saw Hannah go inside with the woman. *I could go back and forth, I suppose, but what if I get caught up in something and can't come back nightly? You wanted me here every night.*

I'm sorry. I guess I figured you…I don't know. I guess I figured you'd work here at something. But…I have to go. Misha is yelling for me. We'll talk later about this, okay? She told him sure. *Have fun. Spend some money and get yourself something. I'll see you tonight.*

She closed the connection and sat down on the little sofa. As she sat there, she reached out and found a few crimes going on but stayed where she was. Linyah was trying her best not to get hurt again.

But when something made Maribel tense up, she focused her energy on her and waited. Maribel had told her to not read her every thought, and she would do as she had asked. To a point. This woman meant the world to her, and she didn't want anything to happen to her.

CHAPTER 6

Maribel was just finishing up her shopping when she felt him nearby. It was all she could do not to abandon her things and simply run. But running would cause a scene and she wasn't going to do that. Instead she rounded the next aisle and turned to look at her ex-husband.

"What do you want?" He stepped closer to her, but she held her ground. "You don't scare me anymore, and you're not supposed to be around me. I think you were—"

"Shut the fuck up." Her mouth snapped closed, but she didn't back away. "I want you to tell them damned boys that you're taking me back. I don't want to have to show you what could happen to you again if you disobey me. I'm your mate. You'd be better off just—"

"No." He lunged for her, but she shoved the cart in his belly. Before she could think about it, she reached for Linyah just as Andy shoved her back. Maribel slammed against a wall of canned goods and the full cart was tipping onto her when she was suddenly set on her feet. She looked into the furious face of Linyah and felt relieved that she was there.

"What the fuck do you think you're doing?"

Maribel nearly sobbed with relief when Linyah turned on Andy. If she'd looked at Maribel the way she was Andy, Maribel was sure she'd be running in the opposite direction. Andy, however, was too stupid to do more than fight, his natural way of doing things.

Linyah turned toward Andy and slapped him in the face. "I asked you a fucking question. What the fuck do you think you're doing? And you'd better have a better answer than you were just looking around. I'll fucking knock you on your ass if you don't."

"You can't talk to me that way. I'm leader here to this leap, and you'll obey me or so help me —"

Maribel almost burst out laughing when Linyah cut him off with another slap to the face. He looked murderous, and Maribel loved it.

"You are nothing, you overgrown piece of shit. Especially to me. Being here frightening Maribel is going to get your ass killed, and I'm just the person to do it. Besides, I thought you were warned not to come here again. And now here you stand pissing me off and hurting this lovely woman." Linyah glanced at her and winked before turning back to her mate. "Next time I won't come here and save your ass but let her rip you a new one. She's going to do it, too, if you keep fucking around."

"Her? You think she has it in her to kick my ass?" He threw back his head and laughed, and Maribel felt her cat stir. But they were in a crowded store and she calmed her with the promise of doing something to the man the next time she saw him. Andy continued as if the thought of her standing up for herself was going to be funny. "She can barely stand up to the postman, much less me. And she's my mate. Don't you know she can't harm me at all?"

"I can." It was Misha who spoke this time, and Thomas was standing next to him. They both looked as if they were going to kill their father, and Maribel started to step between them. But Linyah held her back and told her to stand still. Misha took a step to his dad, and smartly, Andy took one back. "You'd better back off, old man. I'm not in the mood to fuck with you."

"You should know that I'm coming back to this leap and I'm taking over. You've done nothing but let things slide to the shithole that you've lived in all your life. And when I get back, things will be different. And you'll pay me a part of your money too. I'm not doing this without compensation this time."

No one moved, but Misha crossed his arms over his chest. Maribel watched Andy while he stood there. She wondered what he was up to when he turned and walked away. As soon as the automatic door closed behind him, Maribel felt herself sag with relief. Then she looked around.

"How did you get here?" She looked at her sons when neither of them answered. Misha looked at Linyah, and Thomas just stood there staring at them as if he were upset.

"I had them brought here." Maribel looked at her newest daughter-in-law, then at Thomas when he spoke again. "Linyah told me what was going on and the things that Father was saying. She thought it was a good idea if Misha knew first-hand what Dad was planning, and I agreed with her. But if he thinks that hurting you or anyone in this family is going to work for him, he's stupider now than he was back when we were kids."

Maribel nodded her agreement. Andy was never very smart, but he did seem to get dumber as the years went by.

"And he left so quickly because...?" Linyah just shrugged off her question. "I see. I guess I can expect this sort of thing a lot now that you're a part of the family. You being able to take care of a situation without lifting a finger."

"I can, and why shouldn't I if it keeps you safe?" Maribel had no answer for that but looked at Thomas when she did. "I thank you for bringing your brother. We should try to keep your mom from being alone too much, don't you think?"

"I do. And how is the shopping going?" She flushed, and Maribel had a moment to wonder what that was about when Thomas spoke again. "You should go back with Hannah. I'm sure she's wondering what the hell happened to you. That way when you finish, we can talk."

Linyah's face turned red from a surge of anger, but said that Hannah was waiting in the restaurant and that her aunt had not shown before she'd left. Linyah looked at Maribel and winked, then just disappeared. Maribel looked at Thomas, who was frowning. He was upset, but she didn't know why. When she started to ask him, he looked at her and shook his head.

"Not now." She nodded. "I can't...it was too simple for me to do this, bring Misha and me here. Not that I minded to be here for you, but this is just...she's got powers that are fucking scary."

Maribel ignored the bad word. She was more concerned with the fact that he seemed afraid more than anything. And of his mate. She let Misha help her unload the cart while Thomas bagged the groceries for the house.

Nothing else was said until they were out in the parking lot. There was a large man standing by a limo where she'd parked her car, and that made her pause in mid-step. He bowed to them.

"I have orders to return you from where I found you. Your own car is safely at your home." Maribel looked at Misha, then at Thomas when neither of them spoke. "This conveyance will be at your disposal at any time you need it. I can take them to the office." The man bowed again and went to the trunk and opened it, and began to put the things she'd just gotten into the deep yawning mouth of the car. She looked at Misha and Thomas, who simply stood there.

"Are you upset with me because I called Linyah or is it something else?" Misha shifted on his feet and Thomas only stared at her. "Answer me. Are you mad because I didn't call either of you when he showed up?"

"No, I'm not mad at all. I'm pissed at our father." She tried to gauge what mood Misha was in, but he only smiled at her. "She saved your butt and smacked him around a little. Wish I could have seen that. But no, Mom, I'm not mad. Neither is Thomas. He's just trying to get a grip on things, that's all."

Get a grip on what? She could only imagine. His life? Sure that was a part of it. But she had a feeling it was something more, at least more than his father showing up and Linyah coming to help her. She prattled on about nothing, and Thomas still said nothing more. Maribel worried a little. She hoped that he wasn't upset with Linyah, but before she could ask him, Misha kissed her cheek and told her to let it go. She nodded but still worried.

The driver drove them back to the big office that her sons all shared. Maribel didn't go there often but when she did, it was to only pick something up and then leave. And since she had groceries this time, she just stayed in the car to go home. But Thomas didn't get out of the car when Misha did.

"Mom, what am I going to do with her?" She had no idea what he meant but didn't get the chance to ask him before he continued. "She can do all sorts of things that are frightening, and keep you safe when we can't. I get that and I'm glad for it. Father would have hurt you had she not gotten there when she did."

"He could have hurt me with you standing right next to me too. Her being there was because I was thinking of her when he shoved the cart at me. It could have been any of you at that moment." He nodded but didn't speak. "What are you bothered by, son? Is it that you don't want her? Do you think that she's going to hurt you somehow?"

"She's bored." That made her nearly smile, but she held back. "I don't know how to keep her happy if she's bored with me. Today she told me that she wants to continue working for her family. I want her home at night."

"Is she bored with you or simply bored? I get bored too. It's why I do the shopping and go on errands even though they have this big house with servants. I like doing things for myself." He nodded. "Does she want to go on missions with you guys? Have you even asked her what she wants to do? Thomas, you have to talk to her. This isn't right and you know it."

"I do know it. And we're going to talk. But she said she could go and still work with her family and try to get back home to me nightly. I think she'd just rather continue on as if we'd never met." Maribel wondered if that was really it or there was something more.

"Again, did you ask her what she wants to do?" He shook his head. "Then you should. Don't let this fester, son. Go and talk to her and see what she wants to do. Maybe she could find a job around here that she'd enjoy. Or she could work for her family until she finds something. You can't expect her to hang around the house all day. She's a woman who gets things done."

"I don't, not really. And as for her finding something to do? Not unless it involved guns and knives." He laughed, but it was bitter sounding. "And I can't stand how messy she is. Christ, it's like living with a small child. She can't even put the lid on the toothpaste without leaving a trail of paste on the sink."

Maribel smiled at that. She'd heard the story about her and the toothpaste art. She wondered if that was all there was to it and decided that they both needed to be left alone on this. They'd work it out. Thankfully they couldn't harm each other. She thought that before this was finished, Linyah and Thomas would have one of the strongest relationships she'd ever been witness to.

After making his confession, he told her he had to go. Getting out, he turned back and gave her a quick kiss on the cheek. Then he told her he loved her.

"I love you as well." He nodded as he closed the door. She looked at the man who was driving her home. "Who do I have to thank for this sort of service?"

"Queen Kendra, my lady. She heard about your problems today and sent me to care for you until things are settled. She said that if any harm comes to you, I should simply lie down and die. Queen Kendra said she'd be most displeased if you were harmed."

Maribel thought she'd be displeased as well and smiled. This was really the strangest grocery shopping she'd ever done. And the most fun.

~~~

Hannah watched her aunt and noticed not for the first time she was overly tense and she seemed completely distracted. When she glanced at Linyah, she too looked a little out of sorts. She wondered what had happened but said nothing yet. Her aunt had shown up almost immediately after Linyah had. But Linyah did promise that she'd explain later. Lucky for her, she'd contacted Misha and he'd told her what had happened.

"I just don't know why you don't just go and live with them for a time. They are your grandparents. And probably just want to get to know you. I thought you'd jump at the chance to see them. I didn't know you could be so stubborn." Before she could tell her aunt no for what seemed like the thousandth time, she spoke again. "It's not as if you need their money or anything. I mean, just go so that he'll be satisfied."

"But you do, don't you? You do know why she won't go and the reason he wants her so badly." Linyah stared hard at Wanda, who paled. "You've gotten yourself into some deep trouble, and now he's blackmailing you to do just what he wants. You've no choice in the matter, or so you think. What did you think was going to happen when you asked him for a loan? Did you really think he'd just lend you the money and things would be fine?"

Her aunt looked like she'd been a big balloon and someone had stuck her with a pin. Her body sagged, whether from relief or something more, Hannah didn't know yet.

"He said I could just do him a favor some time. A small one he'd said. He said it would be…I'm at his beck and call constantly now. Even in the middle of the night he calls me. I don't know what to tell Daniel. I was so glad that we moved here. I thought he'd just…."

Aunt Wanda started crying and Hannah wanted to comfort her. But Linyah pulled her back and shook her head slightly. She sat still, but she hurt for the woman as she watched her deal with whatever was going on.

"Perhaps you shouldn't gamble. What do you still owe the casino in your town? Nearly ten grand, and you kept going back when they told you that your credit was good. Do you honestly think that you were going to get ahead that way?" Aunt Wanda nodded, her eyes red and swollen. "It wasn't going to happen, not with Little in charge of things. In fact, I would say that you're only going to end up dead if you keep this up."

Aunt Wanda nodded, then looked at them both. Hannah wondered then just how deep her aunt was in this. Gambling was a horrible addiction, and her aunt seemed to have it bad.

"I tried to make it right. I even asked if I could make payments on what I owed. It was as if they knew I have a gambling problem. And…wait a minute. How the hell did you know all that?" Aunt Wanda looked at Hannah, pissed. "You told her? You found out somehow and now you're going to blackmail me too? Well I got news for you, I don't have a damned thing left. My piss pot is so empty right now that it has a crack in the bottom from being so dry."

"I've no reason to blackmail you. I have everything I want or ever need." Hannah huffed at her. "I really don't care if you believe me or not. You've been leading me down a merry path since I met you. I just knew that whatever was going on, my grandfather was behind it. I just...it's why I asked Linyah to come here with me today. Does Uncle Daniel know?"

Wanda shook her head and started to stand.

"Sit down." Linyah's voice was sharp and had she been standing, Hannah would have sat too. Wanda glared but she sat down. "You think that he's going to let you off with whatever he's got you doing with Hannah? You really think that a man like him won't have you on the hook for the rest of your life? You're stupider than I gave you credit for if you think that. The man is an evil, greedy bastard that will suck you dry before he's finished with you."

"He said that if I got Hannah to him, he'd wipe my slate clean."

This time Linyah snorted at her. For some reason, Hannah thought that Linyah had it right. He was going to suck Wanda dry, and her too if she let him.

"All she has to do is go to his house for a period of one month. One fucking month. Is that too much to ask?"

"Yes." They both looked at Hannah when she spoke. "I've never met the man, but I already know that he's not all that trustworthy. And I can't believe you actually believed that I'd simply go to them without taking someone with me, or at least taking some sort of precautions. I have a husband that I love, a lovely home, and—"

"So you're not going to help me." When Aunt Wanda stood this time, so did Linyah. "What do you think you're going to do? Hurt me? I have news for you, it can't hurt me any more than what it's going to do to me to tell my husband. He's the best thing that ever happened to me. I love him with all of my heart and because of this, I'm going to lose it all. Everything in my life, what was good and nice, it's all going to be gone."

"I can help you." Aunt Wanda shook her head at Linyah. "I can. I can even get the men you owe money to back off too. Or to go away altogether. I have a little experience in this sort of thing. I'm very…talented."

"You can't kill them all. And for as much as I dislike the old bastard, I love Carole and don't want her hurt in all of this. But I can't do this anymore." She sobbed a little more, then sat down. "I'm a mess. And even though I've stopped gambling — and I really have this time — I still owe them so much money. So very much. When Daniel finds out, he's going to leave me. And despite his father, I love him with all of my heart."

"What is the name of the casino and the name of the man that you owe?" Aunt Wanda told her, and Linyah nodded to her. "I'm going to make a fast trip. While I'm gone, I want you to explain to your aunt what we are. She has no clue what you are or what you're capable of. My leaving you like I'm going to will help her believe, but you might have to play with your other part just a little to get her to really understand."

Hannah nodded and Linyah disappeared. She looked over at her aunt, who looked like she'd been hit in the back of the head. When Hannah touched her hand, she jerked back so quickly that she spilled the water. She started talking as she mopped up the water with her napkin. Her aunt was in for a huge awakening.

"I'm a leopard. Well, the entire family is. And Linyah is…well, I'm not really sure what she is, but she can do all these amazing things. She's even shared one of them with me. It's how I knew that you were helping my grandfather." She finished with the water just as their salads were being served. As soon as the man left, she continued. "Misha is the leader of the family; it's called a leap, a pack of cats is a leap. Anyway, when I met him he converted me—"

"She's gone." Hannah nodded. "And you can read my mind, like she can. You said that, you can read my mind and know everything about what I've done. You also believe that you're a cat, a leopard. And you can what, change into it when you want?"

"Yes." Her aunt stood up, and Hannah grabbed her arm. She let just enough of her cat go so that she ran along her arm, and her claws extended. Aunt Wanda sat down without taking her eyes off the paw that held her. Hannah let her cat stay where she was as she spoke quietly.

"I can do much more than this, the shifting thing I mean. I just figured out the other day that I can shift in mid-jump too. That's an amazing feeling. And leaping over fallen logs and bushes too." Aunt Wanda shook her head. "You can see right here that what I'm telling you is true. I'm holding onto you with my cat. Would you like for me to shift fully?"

"No, please. This can't be happening." Hannah told her it was. "Why are you doing this to me? Why are you...are you trying to make me lose my mind? That's it, isn't it? You think that if you can make me crazy, then you can...I don't know what. But you can do it."

"Shut up." Hannah felt her face heat a little when she spoke to her aunt. "Just shut up. You've gotten me involved in your mess and I'm trying to help you. But if you really think that I'd have you locked up somewhere, then you aren't paying attention to me. The reason I'm doing this is because you're family. And the one thing that

Misha and his leap have showed me is that family, a good family, is more priceless than the biggest diamond in the world. My...what Bella did to me makes my skin crawl when I think about it. How she'd locked me away for no reason. If you'd just get your head out of your ass, you'd see that I'm trying to help you. Tell me everything you know and we can work this out."

Hannah didn't think she was going to answer her, but she finally seemed to come to some decision. Her aunt started talking almost nonstop.

"He's going to take you and keep you under lock and key until you do what he wants. And mostly all he really wants is you were he can control you. That's his thing, control. You should see the way he treats Carole. Like she's this pet and he has her on the tightest leash. When I spoke to Daniel about what he was doing, he told me that he'd tried to help his mom when he was younger and now...well, he thinks she'd leave him now if she could, but believes she has nowhere to go." Hannah nodded, knowing that was what her granddad wanted. "He's not a nice man. I don't think he has ever liked me, but once he figured out that I was in trouble, he was all over it. I think...I don't know about your grandmother, but I would say she's terrified of him."

"She is." They both looked at Linyah when she reappeared. Aunt Wanda whimpered just a little but didn't try to leave. "The man you owe money to works for Mr. Little. The two of them partnered up just after the place opened. And he has a vested interest in the casino where you were. Did you by chance get an invitation to the place with a free marker?"

"Yes. About five years ago. It came in the mail, certified...are you saying I was set up?" Linyah nodded.

"Why, that bastard. He knew that I had a problem, but years before, long before I met Daniel, I'd been to classes to learn to say no. I even went to Gamblers Anonymous to get over the addiction. And he sucked me back in? What a horrible thing to...he used me."

"I would say that's about right." Linyah smiled and Hannah thought it was the scariest thing she'd ever seen. "And you know what? We're going to take him down."

"How? He's got all the money in the world. Connections everywhere. And I'm not sure, but I think he might have connections with the mob family that has been in the paper lately. The man has his fingers into everything, legal or not." Linyah said that she thought so too. "How are you going to take care of him? I'm willing, but...I've decided that I have to talk to Daniel. I have to tell him."

"You do. Because I won't help you if you don't." Linyah winked at her and Hannah knew that she'd made the right decision in telling her aunt that. "You want mine and Linyah's help, then you tell the truth not just to us but to Uncle Daniel as well. They're his parents. As much as I hate confrontations of any kind, I think this needs to be out in the open."

The rest of the lunch was pleasant if a little tense. Hannah even told her aunt about the baby, and also had to explain to her more about being a cat. Linyah for the most part was very quiet, but Hannah felt it was more her nature than her not enjoying the luncheon. As they left the restaurant, hugging at the door, Linyah asked her if she'd like to go back to the mall.

"The mall?" Linyah nodded and flushed brightly. "Do I even want to know what you want at the mall? Or did you want to go and get another cinnamon roll? Those things are just wonderful, don't you think?"

"I can't do any more sugar today. I'm buzzing now. But Thomas said there was this naughty shop there. He said...he asked me to get something he could tear from me. I think today I might have pissed him off. When I left you, I think I might have made him mad at me again." Linyah turned redder as she continued. "I don't have a clue why he finds that so sexy, but I kind of like it too."

They were there for perhaps ten minutes when they found what they wanted. Linyah went to the dressing room while she looked at some of the other things they had. The lady that had been helping them came up behind Hannah and spoke.

"You're the leap bitch." Hannah turned and tried to hide the fact that she really hated that title but smiled at her all the same. "I'm in your leap. Misha is a great leader."

"He's a great husband too." The woman nodded and smiled. "My sister-in-law is trying on some of the sets you have. She's Thomas's mate. Do you know who he is?"

"I do. And this is my shop. I've never...I don't think I've ever seen any of the Lanning men in here, however. But I know of him. I wonder where...?" She flushed a little when she laughed. "I'll be quiet now. I'm glad you came in. I have toys too if you're interested."

Two hours later they were both overloaded with bags. Linyah had not just gotten several of the pantie and bra sets, but she'd also gotten a few of the more revealing sets as well. Hannah had gotten herself one as well, and was excited about Misha seeing it. But it was the thing in the big bag that she was most happy with. Misha was going to have a cow when he saw that thing.

"Do you know what playing is?" Hannah shook her head as they both sat in the back of the big limo that Misha had insisted that they use. "Thomas said he uses clamps on my nipples, ties me up. Things like that. More sometimes, but it depends on the degree in which you want to play. Does...you don't have to answer me, but does Misha play? Not that it's any of my business. I just don't have a clue what I'm supposed to do."

"No. And it's okay. Misha and I do things and all...I mean, we have a lot of fun in the bed." She blushed, feeling her face heat up. "But he's very gentle with me. Why do you ask?"

"As I said, I don't know anything about it either, but I think that Thomas enjoys it. And I want to please him." That was news to her and almost bordered on too much information. "I don't mean to embarrass you. It's just that I don't...I'm not sure what to do to please him."

Hannah nodded and tried to think what to tell her. "I don't either. Maybe you could look it up on the Internet. I've never not found something that I've been looking for."

Linyah nodded but looked out the window. Hannah had no idea why, but she thought she was depressed. And since she'd met her, she realized that she'd never heard her laugh or even smile all that much that didn't sort of look like she was going to hurt you too. She thought about talking to Misha about it, but decided that maybe she'd talk to one of the other brothers. Maybe she'd talk to Rider. He was very serious like Linyah was, so maybe he'd have something to tell her about bringing Linyah out of her funk.

Once they were home—at Misha and Hannah's home—they sat down and went over what Linyah had

planned for her grandfather. An hour into their planning, not only did Rider show up but also Misha and Carter. Thomas was working on some security things for the house, and the other brothers were getting their gear ready for when the next call came in. They told them what had happened and what was going on with her aunt.

"This is all true? I mean, I have no reason to not believe you, but this is as far out there as I've seen." Linyah nodded at Rider's question. "Then why don't you just call in the police? Let them handle it. We don't do this sort of work. It's out of our league."

"You don't, but I do." Linyah continued working on a list as she spoke to Rider. "You can go on all the rescue missions you want, but this is my project. And frankly, I don't want you helping me anyway. You'll just get your nose out of joint on something I need to do, and I don't want you fucking around getting me into trouble." Linyah didn't lift her head from her list and missed the look on Rider's face. It was so comical that Hannah had to put her hand over her mouth.

"I do not get people in trouble. I keep them from it." Hannah looked at Misha as Rider argued. He was laughing and having a hard time keeping it to himself. "I am the one that plans things to make sure that no one gets hurt or killed. Just call the police and let them take over for now. Why do you want to even get involved anyway?"

"Because I said I would." Linyah stood up and stretched her long, lean body. "You are not to interfere, understand me? I do this my way or you get hurt."

"You're threatening me?" Linyah looked like she was considering it by putting her finger over her lips and thinking. Then she looked at Rider and nodded. "I'll have you know that I'm very good at keeping this family safe. And that includes you."

Linyah didn't take her eyes off Rider as she pulled a long switchblade from her boot. Hannah was impressed at how easily she got it opened and handed it to Rider. He didn't take it but stepped back. With a shrug, Linyah slid it over the length of her arm. The blood, what very little there was, trailed along the cut that disappeared almost as soon as the slice was made. No one said a word as she closed the knife and put it back into her boot.

"Christ." No one disagreed with Rider, and when he sat down, so did Linyah. "Does anything hurt you? I'm assuming that Thomas is the same way."

"Yes. So are Hannah and Misha. Nic is the one that shared with Misha, I with Hannah. I like her." She looked at the woman but said nothing. It scared her that she had this sort of magic in her, but was glad too, for the baby. "Would you like it as well?"

Rider said nothing but stared at her. Carter put out his hand and Linyah took it. As soon as he dropped to his knees, Rider stood up again. But Carter was laughing.

"It didn't hurt. Christ, anything but. It was like...I don't know. Sexual release, I guess. And I feel good." He stood up and looked at them all. "I think we can all benefit from this. I know that when we go out, I for one would like to know that I can heal fast enough to keep working."

Rider sat there and stared at her. Even with all that was going on, neither of them seemed to notice. It was like they were having a staring contest and no one was the winner as yet. But when Rider put out his hand, Linyah hesitated.

"When I share, you will get more. More than Carter or the others will get if they want it too." He nodded. "Do you want to know what you might get from me when we share? You're stronger than the other brothers. Not Misha strong, but close."

"I'll take it." She nodded and put her hand into his. Rider winced but said nothing until she let him go. He sat there squeezing his hand open and closed for several seconds. "What do you get out of this? You can't just share and not take, right?"

"You're mine. Someone that I will trust above all others. You will be at my beck and call at all times." Her grin made him slightly uneasy, but she continued. "Rider, think of yourself as my bitch, and I'm going to ride you like a pony in a carousel."

No, he didn't like this one bit. And when she started laughing, Rider hoped it meant she was kidding; but with her, it was hard to tell. Rider just hoped that someday she'd sit down and explain it to him what she really meant.

CHAPTER 7

Thomas looked around the room again. He wasn't sure what he was looking at until Mike came in with a laundry basket loaded with towels and clothes. Thomas looked around the room again and that's when it hit him. It was spotless.

"You did this?" Mike shook his head and put the towels on the made bed. "So you called in a service? Someone to clean up after her."

"No, sir. I came up here to get the laundry basket this morning and it was like this. I just assumed you did it." Thomas smiled and looked around the room. "I take it you did not."

"No. Maybe she's going to work out after all." He turned to look at Mike when he inhaled sharply. "You have to admit, this is much nicer than the mess she left daily. Or is this room the only one that she picked up in?"

"I have not...no, sir." Mike continued to put things away, then left the room. Thomas had a feeling he was pissed about something, but was too happy with the results of the room to care overly much. He reached for Linyah to thank her, but she was blocking him. Not really concerned, he unpacked his clothing and put things away.

After a quick shower, he went to the kitchen to get something to eat before going to the office again. Mike was not there so he made his own breakfast, cleaned up, and left.

At around ten-thirty he felt Linyah reach for him. It made him nervous, of course, not being used to someone other than his immediately family touching his mind after all this time. But when she spoke, not sounding stressed at all, he relaxed as well.

I'm working here and won't be home. He asked her where here was. *At my family home. My sister has two murders on her hands, and I'm going to help her find the killer. I may be gone for several days. I just thought I'd let you know.*

Can't you come home nightly? I thought that with that popping in and out thing, you could come and go as you please. How hard can it be for you to come here to be in the bed with me? She didn't say anything, so he continued. He knew that he'd sounded whiney and he hated it. It flared his temper just a little. *We're mated now, so it would be nice if we could spend some time together once in a while.*

Still nothing. He wondered if she'd closed the connection between them, but when he said her name, she spoke. *I'm going to work. I can't just sit around the house all day waiting for you to return when you finish with something you and your brothers do. I told you the other day that I was going to work. What do you expect me to do? Sit around your house while you continue with your life? I had one before you barged into mine. And I plan on doing as I please.*

Being gone all night for several days is not acceptable to me. I know that you told me you were going to maybe go and work for your family, but I never assumed you'd actually do it. He could feel her anger, and in turn, it pissed him off as well. *Maybe you should think of finding something closer to home.*

That way you can be home when I get there. It's not that hard to find a job if you look.

I see. What is fair for you isn't for me, is that how it is? Well, Thomas, should I put on a little apron for you too? Cook you a meal? Or would you just prefer me to be naked in your bed? His cock stretched at the thought of her being naked anywhere. *I'm not little Susan Homemaker. I do not play at house for any man. You should have left me alone if that was what you wanted.*

I'm not asking you to be my cook. I want you home at night. I have no idea why you think that's such a horrible thing to want. He realized he was screaming at her. He was also standing up at his desk clenching his fists. When he sat down, Thomas tried his best to get a hold of his temper, but she spoke before he could.

I cleaned up after myself. I wear the clothing you want. I eat what you eat. I cannot give you any more of myself. I need me. If you keep trying to make me into something that I'm not, I'm going to be someone that I hate. Unless that's your plan. Is it? He had no idea what she was talking about and said so. *Of course you don't. You're the mighty Thomas Lanning. The cleanest, neatest person on the earth. And you want everyone, me included, to do just what you say when you say it.*

The connection closed. It sounded to Thomas like she'd slammed a phone down and it rang in his ears. He sat there in his chair for nearly twenty minutes before he picked up a mug to throw it across the room. But thinking of the mess he'd make, he sat it down. Rider came into the office just as he was thinking all women were insane.

"Want some advice about women? It's free and very true I think." Rider nodded and smiled. "Don't find your mate. You will regret it for a very, very long time if you do. Find a cave, hide deep within it, and never come out. Because I have news for you, it's not worth it. Not even the mind blowing sex is worth the insanity that they bring to you."

Rider sat there for several seconds, then threw back his head in a loud laugh. He looked at him twice more and did the same again and again. Thomas wanted to order him to get away from him—he had better things to do than to be made fun of. When he seemed to have some control over himself, Rider leaned back in his chair and smiled.

"I take it she's not working out as well as you thought." Thomas snorted. "I see. Well, did you know that I don't think you're a peach to live with either? You're mostly a pain in the ass. And I don't have to put up with you twenty-four seven. She, on the other hand, has stayed with you a great deal longer than the ten minutes I thought she would. I actually feel sorry for the poor girl."

Thomas didn't say anything. He'd already had one fight today and he didn't feel like getting into another one just yet. Instead of saying what was on the tip of his tongue about his habits, Thomas changed the subject.

"I've been working out the budget we have. I think we need to start charging more for local jobs. As it is right now, we're losing money on them more than we do when a project goes over." Rider only nodded but continued to smile. "Do you think that if we charged the local municipals for mileage, Misha would go for it?"

"No. He wouldn't charge them at all if he had his way. But we need to do something or they'll use us for everything like they have been. And I mean everything. Every time a dog or cat comes up missing, they'll be calling us in. It would be a waste of all our time." Thomas nodded. "She's not coming home, is she?"

"No." He looked around the room. It was as neat as his house. "She cleaned up my room before she left. Then she tells me that she's going to be working and gone for a few days. And then she blows up because I asked her to come home every night. What the hell is she working for? To prove to me that she can?"

"I'll bet you didn't ask her at all, did you?" Rider stood up. He looked like he was going to start laughing again but only shook his head. "Tell me something, Thomas. When you left the other day, to work I mean, did you ask her if she wanted to go or just leave her? Did you even tell her that you'd be gone for a few days, or did you assume that she'd simply deal with it? And then when you got back, who did you call first? Her or Mike?"

"What difference does that make?" Rider didn't say anything and that pissed him off more. "You think that because I do it, it's okay for her to just take off too? I'm her mate. I'm supposed to protect her. And she's all pissed off about me wanting her to cook for me. I never asked her to cook anything at all. What the hell is she talking about?"

"Yeah, hell of a job you're doing, too, in protecting her. Did you know that she's hurt again?" Thomas stood up and reached for her. The wall he hit hurt his head. "I'm guessing that's a no. And also, are you aware that her parents are at Misha's house? They've been there for a couple of days. They didn't want to bother the two of you. As for her working...well, jackass, you should really think before you open your mouth from now on. She was hurt protecting the Genjar citizens from a guy who decided to rob what we call a bank and took several people hostage. He ended up killing a few of them before she was able to go in and subdue him. Kill him, I guess. I just found out that only royalty are the ones with all the power. The other Genjar can heal but they can also be killed. He managed to kill four of them before she was able to stop him. She's also out looking for Timmer. If you ask me, I think you're one fuck up from losing the best thing that ever happened to you. Over what? A few clothes on the floor?"

He wanted to argue, but he had a feeling that Rider was right. He was fucking up big time. Then there was Timmer, the guy her sister had promised her to. He started to ask him who had hurt her and he remembered she'd said something about the murders but nothing more. Thomas tried to reach her again and had to sit down. The pain in his head was making him sick. He had to hold up his hand when Rider came around his desk asking him if he was all right.

"She's blocking me." He heard his brother laugh again and decided that he was going to bring every woman he knew around just to help him find his own mate. "It fucking hurts, damn it. I thought she couldn't hurt me as my mate."

"*We* can't hurt our mate. It's hard to tell what she can or can't do. I would think from the look of you that she can do whatever she wants." He felt Rider back up. "I don't suppose you tried to contact her brother? He might be able to help you."

"No. Christ, I have to rest a minute." He did hurt and wiped at his nose. Blood smeared over his fingers and he closed his eyes. "She's really blocking me."

He heard the door open then close. He figured that either Rider had left him or he'd invited his brothers in to see his humiliation. Damn her for putting him into this kind of situation. But he lifted his head, he was surprised to see Linyah's father sitting across from him. And Rider was gone.

"Your brother thought you could use some help." Thomas nodded. "Linyah can be...she gets her stubbornness from me. Well, most of it. Her mother can be a little stubborn as well. But Linyah has it down to a science. Rider said that she's upset with you about cooking you something. You should know that I don't think she knows how. To cook, I mean."

"She's blocking me." He nodded. "And she is hurt. Do you know how badly? And I thought that when she gave me this power, that she'd not be hurt either."

"What do you know of our kind?" Thomas told him not very much. "Most don't. Most think, as you did, that we were all dead. And it looked like we might have been headed in that direction too. For a very long time. But then we banded together and found that while our numbers were low, we were a fairly young group."

"You're thousands of years old." Nildale nodded and smiled. "I take it that means while young, you don't mean in your mid-twenties or later, do you?"

"No, we're all thousands of years old. A few that are older. And I'm going to tell you something else, we're not from this planet. Kendra and Nic were born in our world, but Linyah wasn't. She's been here her whole life. And we have been having children to repopulate our kind. We can have children for as long as we want. And most do, as a matter of fact. But when Linyah was born, we knew that was enough for us." He leaned back as he continued. "Many years ago we were hunted...like animals, as a matter of fact. Even though we kept to ourselves mostly and didn't cause harm to those that came to seek our help, we were still regarded as something of an oddity. People knew, you see, that we were a species that could heal and create."

"Create?" Nildale nodded. "I don't understand. You could create other beings? Or do you mean something else?"

"Magic. We were the creators of most of the magic that humans as well as a few others use. It was something that we were glad to help with. But then humans decided that we were too powerful, too...I guess rich in our knowledge of what we could do. And they set out to destroy what they did not understand. Because unlike them, ours came to us when we took our first breath and only grew stronger as we used it. Humans...sadly humans used it up, destroyed what little they might have had for no good, and then killed for more. When we refused to help them, the ones that were abusing the power we gave them, they decided to end us. And they nearly won."

"So you went into hiding. Taking care of your own when necessary and leaving us...all of us...to wonder where you'd gone." Nildale nodded and smiled sadly. Thomas sat there wondering what, if any, help this was in dealing with his mate. When he started to ask him, Nildale stood up and moved to the door. "What about Linyah? What do I do about her?"

"Do about her? Why, nothing. She will do what she pleases, when she pleases, because she is not your child. The sooner you stop treating her like one, the sooner you'll be able to work things out. Oh, and I'd stop trying to contact her. The pain will only get worse." Thomas started to object. "You have treated her as a child, Thomas. And have been since you met her. You would punish her for...I believe she said you called her style a pig sty."

He flushed but nodded. "You've seen her messes. You've even commented on how messy she is, but were proud that she could find anything at a moment's notice."

"So I have." Nildale opened the door but didn't go out it. "She is not happy, young man. I believe you call it depressed. I've never seen her as such, moping about because she is saddened by your lack of faith in her, making her keep herself to meet your expectations. Did you ask what she wanted from you?"

He hadn't. Frankly, he'd never thought of it. "She cleaned up my room. Then she left me. She's been hurt and I can't contact her without causing me a great deal of pain."

Nildale smiled. "You sound like a spoiled child. She cleaned *my* room. I can't contact her without pain to *me*. What of her pain? What of her things she's given up to live in your home? Do you think she might be wanting something of herself in your place? Perhaps something that she loves or needs? I think you have been thinking of only how this has changed your life and not what this has done to hers."

"I didn't mean it like that." But he had now that he'd thought of it. Never had he thought of it as their home. As their bedroom. He'd never once taken into consideration that she might want to have a different bedroom, something she might like to eat. Instead he'd been harping on things that he wanted. When he looked up to ask Nildale what he could do now, the man was gone. And Thomas was no closer to figuring out how to contact his mate then he'd been before. But now...Christ now he had a whole set of new problems. He'd really fucked up.

"We have an assignment." He nodded to Misha as he walked by his office. "We leave in ten."

Ten minutes. He had ten minutes to contact Linyah and see how she was and if he could...well, he had no idea what he could do but he had to do something. Thomas decided that he'd been whining long enough. It was time to focus on this relationship. He was pretty sure there was more to it than just sex, incredible as it had been. If they were going to make this work, then it was time to change himself too.

He reached for Nic just as he was climbing into the car to leave for the airport.

I can't talk to you right now. I have something going on.

Call me when you can. When Nic said he would, Thomas tried for information that would keep him from worrying. *Is Linyah all right?*

No. And with that, the connection was closed. And as tightly as Linyah had closed it earlier.

~~~

Kendra sat very still. She wanted to get up and hug her sister to her, but wasn't even sure that Linyah would allow it. It was difficult to talk to her at times and touching her, loving her, was even harder than that. Instead she watched as she suffered through another round of stitches.

"How do you not heal when you have a mate? It is the way of our kind." Linyah growled at her, and Kendra, for whatever reason, thought it was funny. "You sound like the dog we have at the castle. Growling because someone has taken your bone."

"I fucking hurt." Kendra nodded and watched as the doctor who was caring for her sister wiped at his brow again. The man was beside himself in fear. Linyah had tossed the other doctor, an idiot for sure, across the room when he'd told her that she was going to have to suffer a bit longer.

"He's trying his best, but I think you have frightened him." Linyah growled again. "If you think that is helping, you are gravely mistaken. You are making him slower for fear you will harm him again."

Linyah had grabbed this doctor around the throat when she'd asked for something to drink. He'd said politely that he'd rather she waited until…and that was all he'd been able to get before she grabbed him. Kendra had begged her to let him go, and the man stood beside the bed and told her it was because she might need something more for pain, and he feared she'd be sick if she took anything.

Linyah had sat as still as she could, but she'd really been torn apart by the mad man she'd brought in several hours ago. Kendra tried to think of something to get her mind off the pain, and smiled when she thought of her male.

"You and your male, you are getting along nicely now?" Linyah didn't answer, so Kendra continued. "He's very nice. I have not spoken to him as yet other than to be introduced to him, but Mother likes him. So does Father, as a matter of fact."

"Mother likes everyone." Linyah hissed in pain but didn't touch the doctor this time. "He's too controlling. I have to keep my things put away. Do you have any idea how long it takes to make sure things are as neat as he wants them? Half my day is spent moving things that I don't care about enough to give a second thought to in a place that will please him. I don't have time for that shit. I have a job."

Her scream had Kendra standing up. That's when she got a good look at what her back looked like. Dizziness had her grabbing for the table that had been rolled next to the bed when the doctor came in.

"He tore you open." Linyah didn't answer, and Kendra moved closer to the bed. She'd been told that Linyah had been hurt and that she needed to be stitched together, but not how extensive the wounds were. She looked at the doctor.

"I'm...she has passed out again, my lady." Kendra nodded and asked him if this was the worst of her wounds. "No, my lady. Her belly was opened to her intestine. Her left arm was nearly torn from her body, as well as her left leg sustained major damage when the man took a whip to her. The major wounds have healed themselves to where she will not lose any more blood, but she is in terrible shape. I fear for her."

"I do as well. But why is she not healing?" He said he didn't know. "I thought that with a male in her life, she'd heal faster and would not be harmed as badly."

"He has not accepted her." Kendra turned to her advisor Libby. "He has mated with her, bonded too in the way of their kind, but he thinks of her more as a problem than someone he will spend his life loving. Her wounds will never heal so long as she is not a part of his life, a part of his heart."

"Why has he...? I don't understand. He has taken her but not into his heart?" Libby nodded and handed her a thick file. She looked at the first few pages before looking up. "What is this?"

"Notes he has left her. I have...I have taken it upon myself to collect them when he writes them. I do not believe Lady Linyah has seen all of them. But the few that she has, she was most hurt by them."

Clean up the toothpaste. Put lid on said tube of paste. Screw the lid on the shampoo bottle so that it's tight. Hang towel on drying rack, not the shower rod. If you are the last out of the bed, make it. The lists were long and sounding more and more sarcastic as they went. When Kendra looked at the last two, her blood boiled over and she handed the file to Libby.

"I would be pissed too if he left me a note not only explaining where the dirty socks go, but including pictures of each item as well." Kendra looked down at her sister as the doctor continued to work, but at a faster pace now. "She's not happy, is she?"

"Nay, my lady, she is not. I have seen her upset before, even angry to the point of murder, but I have never seen her so unhappy." Libby nodded toward Linyah. "Shall I send for her male?"

"I don't think so. He is not to see her unless I approve. If he's allowed to come here by anyone other than me, I will have the head of the person who disobeyed me." Libby looked shocked, then smiled. "She will not be bothered with a male that treats her this way."

"Yes, my lady. I will ensure that your orders are carried out." As she left her, the doctor said he had done all he could.

"She will not fall ill again, will she?" He paled and took a step back. "You do know what I've done to the other who would dare to harm what is mine?"

"I do, my lady, I do." He swallowed hard before continuing. "I have made sure that all of her wounds are cleaned and that each stitch is carefully put in place. She will heal nicely, though I'm thinking very slowly."

Kendra left the man there with orders to call her as soon as Linyah woke. A talk between them was well overdue, and she was tired of walking around on egg shells. As she made her way to her rooms, Kendra was thinking of all the times her sister had cut her out of her life. She knew that she'd done the same, and even being queen was no reason for them to have drifted this far apart. As children they'd been inseparable. Now...now they were like strangers. When a man stepped in front of her, she nearly screamed but then saw who it was. With her hand over her pounding heart, she smiled at him.

"Timmer, you scared me. I have had people looking for you. Didn't you get my messages?" He nodded and smiled. But Kendra had a feeling he wasn't all that happy. "You should go now. I don't have time at the moment to talk to you but soon. Someone should contact you.... How did you even get into the castle walls?"

"I came for you to give me what I was promised. I don't like to be lied to, my lady, and you have done that. You told me that she'd be mine and now she's with another." Kendra started to tell him what she'd done for him. She'd paid all his debts off, which was the real reason he wanted to marry Linyah. She'd given him money for his sisters' educations. Kendra also had made sure that his family had all the health benefits that she and her family had. But before she could tell him, he pulled out a long blade. "I will cut your head from your shoulders if I do not get her for me. I want her now. You made a promise, and I will be given my due."

The blade sliced out and she felt her body ripple with the pain. He'd cut her arms, belly, and hip. The blood poured from her almost as quickly as she healed. But she was weak, and he must have known it. Before she could summon the guard to help her, he hit her in the head. Blackness swallowed her up.

CHAPTER 8

Linyah opened her eyes to see not just her mother but her father, Misha, and Nic. She knew that something had happened. Sitting up, she cried out in pain but didn't let it slow her. Misha was helping her lay back down before she could think he shouldn't be touching her.

"What's happened?" Her father turned to her, and she could see the tears on his face. Her dad was a strong and powerful man. And if something brought this much sadness to him, then she wasn't sure she wanted to know what had happened. "Dad?"

"Kendra is missing. We…there was a note, but we've not been able to figure out where he's taken her." She asked who. "Timmer. He talks about how she'd made a promise and now she was going to take it back. He is most angry. He hurt her too. The man is going to pay for this. If it's the last thing I do, I'm going to make him pay."

Linyah started to rise again, but Misha pushed her back to the bed. "You do that again and I'll make you regret it every time you have to take a piss. My sister is missing and I mean to find her."

He grinned at her but said nothing as she stood up. If there was a place on her body that didn't hurt, she didn't think it was doing a wonderful job of hiding from her. As she moved slowly to the smallish room that served as a bathroom, she started talking. It was that or sob.

"When did this happen?" No one answered her, so she looked at Nic. "When did she get taken? Get me details I can work with. I'm assuming that a lot of time has passed while you let me sleep?"

"Yes. She was taken three days ago." Linyah nodded, waiting. There was more; she'd bet her life on it. "She was cut badly, I would say, from the amount of blood that was left behind. And when he left with her, he killed two of her royal guard as well as injuring Libby. She's the one that called us. Otherwise we might not have gotten a start when we did. And we have everyone out looking for her."

"And just what sort of start do you have?" She wanted to ask where Thomas was, but she guessed he was thrilled to not have her at his house. Instead she continued to ask questions of Nic as the rest stood around. When she moved into the bathroom to change into her uniform, Linyah looked at herself in the mirror.

She was a mess. Not just that, but she looked like she'd been run over several times by a large stone and then flipped over to be run over again. The stitches were clean and neatly put in, but there were too many of them for her to count. The murderer had done a number on her before she'd been able to kill him. Turning her back to the mirror over the sink, she finished dressing and then moved out of the room to see that everyone but Misha had left.

"Funny thing about this mind reading thing Nic gave me...I can read everyone's but his." She didn't say anything to him as she limped slowly to the chair. "You're wondering about Thomas. What would you like for me to tell you?"

Linyah pulled on her boots. It was slow going and so painful she wanted to cry, but she finally got them on. Lacing them up was impossible, so she left them hanging open with the laces stuffed into the top of the leather. She leaned back in the chair and looked at Misha when he laughed.

"He is well and happy, I'm assuming." Misha nodded. She also figured that he was pissed. "I have not messed with his things in several days, and I did clean up before I left. If he is angry about that, then it isn't my fault. It's been three days. Tell him to get over it."

"I read the notes he left you." She nodded. She had seen them all despite Libby stealing them from the house when she didn't think she'd notice. Linyah knew it was her and that she was more than likely giving them to her sister, and they were both getting a big laugh out of them. It would be just like them to bind them into a book and sell simply because her sister was queen. "There was no cause for that, and I told him so. If you'd like to know what I said to him, then ask. I'll be more than happy to give you a blow by blow of what transpired between us."

"I really don't want you interfering into what happens between the two of us. And I don't need you to help me, Misha. I'm a big girl who can care for herself." She didn't look at him when he made an odd noise. She pretended to be interested in the lint on her uniform. Thomas did that as well, a cross between a growl and a snort. "What goes on between your brother and me is private."

"Not when it is at the cost of hurting one or both of you." She didn't know why he even cared and said so. "Because as much as you make him pissed off, you amuse me. And you're a part of my leap. And Hannah thinks the world of you." She liked the young bitch too. And wondered if she was okay too. But instead of entrenching herself into their lives more when she might be leaving them, she stood up.

"I have to find my sister." She started for the bedside table to get her gun and nearly sobbed when she noticed he was standing there looking like a man who would fight her. "If you raise your fists to me, I will get back at you. I may not be in the best of shape, but I will heal sometime and then I will—"

"I have told him that he will no longer be welcome in my leap if he doesn't treat you as he wants to be treated. There will be no more notes such as the ones he's been leaving you. And he will not order you about like you're five." She sat down, not sure what good that was going to do. "You should have come to me when you got the first one. It's not right that he did this in the first place. Mom didn't raise him to be an ass."

"Come to you? For what?" He sat down too. "What would you have been able to do? Make him like me? No thanks. I have people who are made to like me and she hates me all the more for it. And I think this arrangement will work out better for the two of us. I'll see him when he needs to have sex and leave his things alone."

"Your sister loves you very much." She shook her head at him. "You're wrong if you think otherwise. I don't think Kendra hates you. I think...from what I've heard around here lately, I would say that she's in awe of you."

"Awe? What are you drinking? Awe? She...she's queen and I'm a lowly princess. One who is nothing like her, not worthy of her time unless she needs something from me. It's better for us both, her and me, if you just leave this alone. And the thing with your brother. I will...I have decided to do what is necessary to keep him safe."

"At what cost to you?" She didn't answer. "Do you know why you haven't healed? It was my understanding that when you found your male, you became invincible. You'd heal quickly and not be down when someone hurt you. But you're not healing like he does. Do you know why?"

"What does it matter?" She knew why. He didn't want her, and until he accepted her into his heart, then she was no different—in fact, worse off—than she'd been before she'd met him. "I will heal."

"You love him, don't you, Linyah? And if it's not love, then you have accepted him as a part of you. Is that right? You've accepted him as your other half?" She nodded. "Do you love him?"

"No. But he is my male and that's all that's necessary." Misha nodded and stood up. "What concern is this of yours? I have done nothing to warrant you coming here. I'm hurt, yes, but I have been before. My sister is missing, but that is really no concern of yours either. What possible reason could you have for coming here and telling me this stuff?"

"You, as I have said before, are a part of my leap. And as Thomas's mate, you are also my sister-in-law. I care for those who matter to me." He laughed when she told him to fuck off. "That might work with some of the men who work with you, but I know you better. You're very hurt by all this and I'm going to help you fix it."

"I don't want your help. And you have no reason to feel any obligation toward me. We have made our lives what they are and will learn to live with it. What does it matter?" He said nothing as he moved to the door. "What are you going to do about him, Misha? Order him about as he's done to me? That will not make him accept me."

"No. I'm not going to do anything. I will...Hannah wants me to tie the two of you together and lock you in a room with a large bed. But I don't think that will work. The two of you have no issues in that department." Her face heated, and he smiled. "I didn't think so. But I will do nothing. Not unless I have to."

She didn't know what that meant but said nothing. As soon as he left her she leaned back in the chair and reached for her sister. No one, not even her sister, knew that she could reach for anyone she wanted no matter where they were or who they were. When she felt Kendra's weakness and pain, Linyah knew that no matter what she'd have to find her.

Do you know where you are? Kendra tried to hide her pain, but it was only making her weaker. *Don't do that. You're only making yourself weaker, and a weak queen is a dead one. You have to let me find you. If you want, you can tell everyone that you got out on your own rather than tell them I did it.*

I love you. Linyah felt her heart take an unexpected twist at her sister's words. *I love you so very much. And if you'd be so kind as to come and get me, I'll show you just how much.*

You don't have to tell me that, Kendra. I'll still come and —

Shut up, you stubborn fool. I love you. And I'm sorry for whatever I did to you to make you hate me. Before she could tell her she'd done nothing, Kendra continued. *I've been a horrible queen, a terrible person, and the worse sister in all of the worlds. I shouldn't have interfered in your life. I should have...I'm so proud of you. And all that you do for me. I've never...I've been so jealous of you since the day you transported us from our room to the swimming hole when I was thirteen.*

You said you wanted to play. Linyah felt her laughter and smiled. *I need to come and get you. Do you know where you are?*

I'm not sure. But we're close to a town. He brings me food and he's not gone long. Have you heard of a place called Marco's? They have this thing called a pizza. Linyah told her she knew where it was and what a pizza was. *It's not...I don't think I care for it overly much, but he really likes it.*

What kind have you tried? Linyah was trying to distract her sister when Thomas was suddenly standing in front of her. She turned her back to him as she continued talking to her sister. *I'll be there soon. I have to wait until he comes back in to follow him. Will you be able to hold on for a bit longer?*

Yes. Linyah, we're going to have to talk when I get back. I mean...I've messed up so much between us, all I can think about is how this is all my fault. I should have let you live the way you wanted. Linyah said nothing but turned when Thomas said her name. *Do you have company?*

Yes. Thomas is here. I'm assuming that Misha sent him. Her sister laughed. *This is not a situation that you should be involved in right now, if ever. What I want you to concentrate on is trying to think where you are and the bath you're going to need when you get here. I've been around Timmer. He stinks. I will come for you soon.*

"Hello." She didn't say anything to Thomas when he spoke, but she did nod her head. "I've just figured out how to pop in and out of this place. I had no idea it was that easy. I mean, it was at home, but here? Had no idea."

"I'm very busy." He nodded but didn't leave. "Seriously, if this is about anything I've done to your home, I'll fix it when I get ba—"

"I was wrong to do that to you." She didn't say anything, and he stood there. "You're very pissed, aren't you?"

"No." He raised a brow. "I'm not pissed. What would be the point in using that sort of energy for something that would get me nowhere? I simply don't care any longer. You have your life and I'm going to make one for me. One that doesn't involve you and your neat freak lifestyle."

"My mother is really pissed off. And Hannah won't speak to me. They think I'm a fool." Linyah wondered if he expected her to say he wasn't, but she couldn't lie to him. "I am a fool."

"What is it you want from me? I've done what you've told me. But I'm not going to be...I can't live with you full time. When you want sex or something we can do it, but I can't live with you. Not and not want to kill you every minute of every day." He nodded and sat down. "I have to go. My sister needs me."

"I understand that. But you can listen to me for a second. I would like for you to listen to me for a second, please. I want us to start over." She shook her head and he nodded. "Please? I want us to...I would like for you to give me another chance."

"At what?" Her body was betraying her and rather than fall on her face, she sat down. "What do you think us starting over can do for this? Nothing. You have your own way of doing things and I can't live with that. It's as simple as that. I'm too old to be expected to change overnight. And that's just what you want. Perfection. I'm not that."

"You are, I just never noticed it before. And I can't live without you." She started to tell him he'd get over it when she messed something up of his again, but he continued.

"I miss you in the house. I miss waking up next to you, smelling you in the house — our house — when you're moving from one room to the next. Mike said that you have him trying some of the things you eat here. He made me paltate last night, and all I could think of was sharing it with you."

Her favorite dish. It was made with fresh lobster and shrimp, baked in a clay pot until it was done. Then lavender and rice was put with it that had been cooked in another pot. Carrots and paltate, a small tuber that tasted like a mixture of potato and squash was put with it all and served on a sizzling pan. Her mouth watered just thinking about it. But she had to go and stood up. As soon as she did, she felt the difference immediately.

"What are you doing?" He shrugged but didn't move. "You can't want me in your life. Take it back. I just don't have time for you being an idiot right now."

"I don't think it's possible for me to take it back. Even if I wanted to." He stood up too and moved slowly toward her. She might have backed up a little, but the chair she'd been sitting in blocked her. "I want to touch you. I want to...I know you have to go to find your sister, but the thought of laying you over that bed and holding you in my arms for all eternity makes me sad to see you go."

"It's just sex, Thomas." He shook his head. "Then I don't understand. What do you want of me? I don't have anything else to give you."

"I want you to love me. Forever. I want you to take me into your heart as I have done and love me forever. Please?" She didn't answer him but felt his fingers glide over her arm. The hair there danced, and her blood heated. "I've been falling in love with you all along. I've been...I think that fighting with you, shoving you away, was a way for me to not admit that it was happening. I didn't want my life to change, and I was blaming you for it."

"You don't know me enough to love me." His lips moved over her throat and she moaned. "I don't have time for this."

"I know." But he didn't stop. In fact, he nipped at her throat so hard that she had to hold onto him or fall. "I love the taste of your skin. The way your body comes to life when I touch you. I especially love when you're aroused and you perfume the air with your scent."

He took a step back, and she staggered slightly. Her body was on fire. And he was the only way to put it out. Just as she reached for him, she felt her sister touch her mind. This time there was desperation in her voice.

He's back and he's going to hurt me again. Grabbing onto Thomas, she took them to the restaurant. She didn't waste any time in finding the man who had served Timmer, but pushed her way into his mind to see what he knew. Not a lot but it was something to go on. As soon as they stepped into the street, Thomas pulled her into the alley and shifted.

I have his scent, remember? The day in the field he and I came close enough together so that I can smell him. I can find him this way. She nodded and touched his fur. *Christ, do you have any idea how much I want you to run right now? Let me chase you down, take you to the ground then fuck you like my cat wants to?*

"I need to find my sister." Thomas asked her for the hand she'd touched the man in the restaurant with. As soon as he licked her, she wanted to beg him to take her then.

You're going to be fucked so hard when we get back to our house. I'm going to tie you to my bed and eat you from head to toe. Then I'm going to start over again as my cat. Her breath caught, she was so needy. *Follow me. The sooner we get this over with, the sooner we can go home and play.*

~~~

The going was rough. He was going up what was essentially a rock-covered mountain without much in the way of purchase for his cat to leap over things. Thomas knew that finding her sister was going to mean so much more than simply helping her. It was going to be the beginning. Linyah in his life, them being there for each other, was going to be the best thing that ever happened to them. When she told him to stop, he did. His body, his cat was on high alert. When she pressed her body to the rocky surface where the scent was, he did the same.

"Someone is coming. I think...I don't know the scents of all your family yet as cats. Can you reach out and see which one it is before I kick his ass?" He lifted his nose to the air and nearly laughed when he realized who it was. Andrew and Rider were coming from the south of them. "There are more."

They were all there. Not just his brothers, but Nic too was moving closer to where they were. He nearly told him to stop. They were messing with his trail when Misha held up his hand. No one moved. Nic, a big man, looked back at his brother as he started to use the hand language that they'd developed when they had started working together. Each of them shifted, and Nic nodded before he, too, shifted into a large leopard. Christ, they were scary and he knew them all.

He heard Linyah say something that sounded like "show off," but they were moving around the trail and toward them now. He watched, and Misha, usually the one in charge, nodded at Thomas to take direction. He felt his pride in his brother go off the charts. The man was the best leader he'd ever known.

His scent is strongest here, but it's fading quickly. I don't know if he went up the hill or turned south from here. Andrew took off straight ahead of them and Phillip to the left. *He's carrying a large cheese pizza and a salad. I think he's taking it to Kendra.*

"He is." Thomas looked at Linyah when she spoke to them. "Kendra said she's in a cave, but it's not really dank or dark like she'd thought. There's power, but she doesn't think that Timmer brought it in. Does that help?"

It does. Misha nodded to Rider, who went to the right of them, followed quickly by Nic. *There's a silver mine about a mile that way. If he has power, it's more than likely there. What else do you have? I'm assuming you're able to talk to your sister and she's helping us find her?*

"Yes. I could always talk to her or anyone whenever I wanted. It mattered little where they were, too. She's hurt but not badly. Pissed off that he's eating pizza and he's feeding her a salad. When this is over, she wants one that has all meat and a stuffed crust." Linyah laughed. "She also wants a glass of soft drink. My sister isn't really a woman of the world, I guess you could say."

Done. Misha looked up the hill before he said anything else. *I think, for the time being that is, that you should stay back as much as possible. You're still weak and could be —*

"I'm going too." He looked at Linyah hard, then at Thomas. "He has no say in this. She's my sister and —"

He said that if I stopped you from going, I'd have to deal with him. Not true, but Thomas would have fought his brother had he tried to stop her from helping. He thanked Misha for his understanding. *Anytime, little brother.*

Darkness was falling fast, and they couldn't find Timmer's scent any longer. As they made their way across the mountain for what seemed like the millionth time, Thomas caught something in the air. He lifted his head and nearly cried out with relief when he smelled fresh urine. Calling the others to him, Thomas leaned into Linyah when she sat down hard. She was exhausted and not going to last much longer in her weakened state.

I can smell him. He's just taken a piss. Thomas looked at Linyah, who was staring at him glassy eyed. This time he spoke only to her. *Please let me do this for you. I can find her and bring her to you as soon as we take care of this. You're not well enough to be taking on this man, and it could get one of the rest of them hurt. Please, let me help you.*

I need to be sure she's all right. She told me that she loves me, and I have to be sure it's not a joke. He nodded but didn't stop rubbing his head on her arm. *I can't move. My body is straining now just to keep upright.*

Stay here. I'll bring her to you, I promise. Even if I have to put her over my back to do so. She nodded and he knew how hard that was for her. Linyah was always strong, but her body had been through a great deal lately. He hurt for her. When she lay back on the ground, Thomas licked her face. Linyah was asleep before he left her.

As they approached the cave, he saw Nic and the rest of them line up behind him. Even Misha stayed back so that he was the first to enter. It was something that he did when someone knew more about a situation than he did. It didn't happen often, but Misha knew that to go in unprepared was to get one or all of them hurt.

Not for the first time, he wondered why Kendra didn't save herself and had meant to ask someone about it. With all their magic, surely they could get out of something as mundane as being kidnapped. But the moment he saw her, he knew. Silver affected her kind as it did most paranormals. She was wrapped up in it like a worm in a cocoon, and she seemed to be in a great deal of pain and unable to heal from it. Timmer was standing near an opening in the cave, this one set back far enough that Thomas had nearly missed him. But when he turned, his body silhouetted against the fire, Thomas knew that the man was insane. His eyes looked like those he'd seen on madmen when they'd been caught in the midst of a horrific crime.

CHAPTER 9

Kendra looked up from her chains and nearly wept with joy. They had come for her. She looked at each of them and was disappointed to not see her sister. But Nic was there at least. When the big cat in the front nodded at her, she nodded back and waited. She tried her best not to move, but her body hurt so badly it just wanted relief. Then Timmer spoke.

"You think you can take me on and get her?" Kendra knew that at some point Timmer had gone over the edge of sanity. He'd been babbling to himself for the last several hours. And yesterday she'd noticed that he'd been answering himself as well. She almost felt sorry for him. But not any longer. She wanted him to pay for all that he'd done. Not just to her but her family as well.

The big cat only nodded and moved deeper into the cave. Kendra wondered why they didn't rush him, but stopped from asking when her brother touched her mind.

He does not see all of us yet. If young Thomas can get him to give up without harming him, we'd rather it happened that way. Thomas believes him to be sick in the mind. She wondered again where Linyah was, and Nic spoke again. *She is weak. Very much so. Healing nicely now that the young cat has spoken to her, but not well enough to be here. She has*

135

only just lain down. I don't think she would have made it had she had to fight with Timmer for you.

She will be all right then? He told her she would be when she had some proper rest. *She'll get it even if I have to tie her down.* Nic laughed.

She will get it if the young cat has any say in it. And you, my dear sister, will let him have his way about this. They are going to work this out and should be left alone to do so. Kendra watched Thomas as he moved around the cave. Her body burned, but she still watched as the cat moved with Timmer as if they were doing a dance that only the two of them understood. When Timmer pulled out a gun and pointed it at her, she watched as Thomas stood in front of her. He was protecting her with his body.

Kendra, when I tell you to, I want you to look away. She nodded when Thomas spoke to her, then realized he couldn't see her. Telling him she would, he thanked her. Kendra wondered what was going to happen when he told her now and leapt at Timmer. The man fell back as the cat took him to the ground.

The screams were cut off. The scent of blood filled her nostrils as she turned away. A shot was fired, then another, but Kendra didn't look back. As much as she wanted to see that Thomas was okay, she didn't want to see him covered in his own blood. Nic moved toward her as a man and she sobbed out her relief. The other cats, Thomas's family, moved into the cave as well, each of them shifting to men. And like Nic, they were fully dressed as they helped unchain her.

Nic lifted her into his arms when she was freed. He'd turned them so that she couldn't see what was in the dark part of the cave, and she was grateful for that. Thomas asked her if she would mind seeing Linyah before she left, and she looked at Nic. Her thoughts were that her sister would come back to their home with her.

"She's my mate, Kendra. And I'll care for her. But she wants to see you." Kendra was torn. She wanted to care for her sister, but knew that she couldn't. Nodding once, she was carried out of her prison to a small clearing not twenty yards from where she'd been held. Her sister was lying so quietly and still that she was afraid for her.

"Hi." Linyah smiled up at her but made no effort to sit up. That worried Kendra very much, but she didn't comment. "You should know that you're projecting your fear very loudly. I'm fine. Only exhausted."

"You should take better care of yourself." Linyah nodded but smiled. "I'm so sorry. For everything that's happened between us. I never knew...I had no idea what to do when you left to hunt. So I did what I do best. Became a bitch and hurt you. It was never my intention to do more than protect myself when I was lonely."

"It wasn't just your fault, you know. I could have been a lot nicer. Or less of a bitch too. But I'm going to be fine. I need a nap is all." Linyah closed her eyes, and Kendra touched her finger to her sister's forehead. It cost her a great deal to heal her, but it would be worth it to argue with her about it. Telling Nic she was ready to go, she moved to her kingdom and into the waiting arms of her mother. Her dad was there as well.

After being fed and pampered for an hour, she found herself in her bed and was just closing her eyes when Linyah touched her mind again.

I'm feeling a good deal better if not just a little tired still. But I'm going to see you tomorrow. We'll have lunch at the pizza place here in town. Have a pop and some ice cream if you're up to it. Things Kendra had wanted to try. *I'm going to be fine; there was no reason to heal me.*

There was every reason. You'll need your strength to play with your mate. Kendra laughed when Linyah growled. *Go and have fun with your male. You deserve it.*

Kendra closed her eyes. She wasn't really that tired, but she knew that tomorrow she needed to look her best. She was having lunch with someone very dear to her and she needed to feel good about herself. Kendra rarely felt good about much when it came to herself. Smiling, she fell into a deep sleep.

~~~

She watched him pace the room. Linyah looked around, wondering what was out of place, but as far as she could see, everything was right where it should have been. When he stopped moving and looked at her, she wanted to beg him to come to bed with her.

"Do you have any idea how terrified I was when I found out you were hurt?" She wasn't sure how to answer him so she didn't. "And they told me that I wasn't allowed to see you. Said that your sister made it so that no one but her could give permission for me to see you. What's up with that? Was she trying to piss me off?"

She had no idea and told him so. "But you got in. How did you manage that? You didn't get past the guard. Had you tried, they would have put you in irons and you'd still be there. What did you do?"

"I told them that if anything happened to your sister, you'd be in charge. What did they think was going to happen when you were queen and I was your king?" She nodded and laughed. "I think that doctor you have there is more afraid of you than he is of Kendra. He nearly begged me to see you when I told him why I was there."

"More than likely. I was...I don't do well when I'm in pain and he was making me hurt in ways that made the original wounds hurt more." She watched him as he stood over her. "You're very far away. I thought you were going to eat me."

"I am. I'm just trying to figure out how to do this. Do I let my cat have you first, or do I take you and let him have you second?" Her body heated at his words. "You're very wet, aren't you? I can smell you, and there's a thick blanket between you and my nose. Show me, Linyah, show me how wet you are."

She pulled the sheet off her body. As soon as she was able, she had taken a shower and was glad now that she'd used some of the pretty smelling creams that she'd bought at the mall that day. She was also glad that she'd not bothered with dressing after. As the sheet fell off her breasts, she watched his face. Thomas looked hungry.

"I've been thinking about you eating me." He nodded but didn't take his eyes from the sheet as it moved down her body and over her. "I thought if you ate at my pussy until I came, then I would be ready for your cock. But if you want your cat to take me first, I know that I'll come hard and my body will be ready for you anyway. Either of you taking me is going to have me screaming, and I can hardly wait."

"He wants to drink from you. Fuck you with his tongue, lapping at your pussy until he gets his fill." She pulled the sheet off her hips and let it fall to the floor. He growled low at her when she opened her thighs for him to see how wet she was. His shift from human to cat was breathtaking, and she watched as he leapt onto the bed with her.

Burying his big head between her legs had her crying out. It hardly registered in her mind that he was an enormous cat and her a simple person. But when he licked her from gate to clit, she curled her fingers into his fur and held on, sure she was going to fly away. Linyah felt her juices flow as he slid his tongue into her and fucked her quickly, his tongue darting in and out of her like she wanted his cock to do. She came three times before she begged him to take her. Looking down her body, she watched as the cat was seemingly swallowed up by Thomas as he lay there.

"Come again." Thomas spread her nether lips open and told her again to come. She wasn't sure she could do it, but he blew over her sensitive clit and she came hard, screaming loudly over and over. As she felt her body relax a little, Thomas pulled her clit into his mouth and bit her. This climax took her breath away.

He ate her over and over as he fucked first her pussy with his fingers then entered her ass, curling his fingers around to stretch her for him. He never stopped lapping at her until she didn't think she'd be able to take much more. Then he sat up, his body hard and glistening with his sweat. As he fisted his cock, a pearl of his cum dripped from the tip, and she licked her lips.

"I'm going to fuck you." Nodding, she started to pant, the thought of him taking her making her dizzy with need. "Turn over. I want to fuck you from behind, take you like my cat would, then mark you."

Scrambling over the bed, she was on her knees when he slapped her ass. The pain seemed to go right to her pussy and she nearly came. As he spanked her twice more, her body heated as she waited for him to do it again. Then suddenly, he lifted her up by her hips and slammed his cock deep into her.

Thomas stilled for just a moment. Linyah wanted to beg him to fuck her, tell him she'd do anything, anything at all for him to move deep within her. But he leaned over her, his cock digging deeper into her pussy as he did so. When he braced his arms on either side of her shoulders, he began to move, slowly at first. His cock moved as if he had all the time in the world.

Her body screamed for relief. Her need to come was just at the edge, blurring her vision and making her heart pound in her chest. When he licked a path from her shoulder to her neck, she tensed up, ready for whatever he gave her, needing everything he was willing to let her have. The bite was more than she could have hoped for. She knew for as long as she lived, she'd see the mark and know that he was hers.

Linyah knew that he'd let a little of his cat go. The teeth that tore into her skin were sharper, longer than his human teeth. As he jerked his head, tearing open her flesh, Linyah felt that this mark would be different than any he'd given her before. This one would never disappear, never fade. It was his mark of ownership, a mark that meant more than a simple taking, but something that would be theirs forever. She would forever belong to Thomas Lanning.

Come. His command echoed in her mind. Her body, belonging to him as surely as it did her, obeyed. Screaming out her release, she felt the darkness slide over her as he tore at her once again, ripping open her shoulder once again. His roar, loud and piercing, bounced around the room, then settled gently almost over her until she was blanketed in it.

~~~

The thought of leaving her made him delay leaving the house. He should have left over five minutes ago, but he'd enjoyed watching her sleep so soundly that he only made a half effort to pack. When Misha asked him for the third time if he was coming, Thomas finally told him he was going out the door now. Leaning down, he kissed her on his mark and left the note for her.

"Contact me when you wake," was all it said. Then he'd signed it, "I love you very much." Thomas was out of the house and into his car before he thought about what she'd think about him telling her he loved her. He did, but the feeling had been so fresh, so new to him that he'd written it before thinking that she might not welcome his love just yet. But he didn't start over with the note as he'd thought about doing. He'd left it for her so she'd know.

As they boarded the plane, Rider sat next to him. He and Rider normally sat at opposite ends of the plane, but today…well, today, it was almost comforting to have him there. They were cleared of the ground and above the clouds when Rider spoke to him.

"Do you take back what you said about me finding a mate?" It took him several seconds to remember what he was talking about. "I'm thinking that you've not just changed your mind, but you now want the world to find their mates. Is that true, little brother?"

"That would be about right." Rider nodded and Thomas continued. "I told her this morning. In a note. I told her that I loved her. I know that it's lame to tell someone you love them in a note like a teenager, but she looked so peaceful laying there sleeping that I didn't want to wake her."

"And the way she is a slob, a messy slob? You can live with that too?" Thomas smiled and nodded. He'd left his own mess this morning. Their clothing was in shreds all over their bedroom and he found that he kind of liked it. "I can see this spoiling a great deal of our fun with you. If you become a slob too, what will we do for entertainment? Moving things around has been the best time we've had as a family."

"Find someone else to pick on? Or I know, just grow up?" Thomas laughed and knew that for the first time in a very long time, he really was happy. "I'd say pick on Carter, but he's not nice when he's picked on. Payback to him is painful."

"You know it." Rider sat there for a little bit longer before he spoke again. "Kendra asked me to tell you something. She said…she wants to know if you could find your way to come to their home. Not right away, but often…visit often. She wants to mend the bond between her and Linyah."

"I don't know why not. I want them to get along better too. It's difficult when you're mad at the one person in the world who can be there for you no matter what." Misha stood up and started handing out files as Rider nodded his agreement. It was going to be a sticky mess they were going into today. The building that had been used for storage of plastics caught fire while over two hundred employees were inside. They were still missing about thirty, five of which were board members as there had been a meeting. They'd been called as soon as the alarm was set and on their way to the fire within thirty minutes of the fire stations being rolled out.

"It's not a simple case of rescue here. The building is still hot they think, and this is from the aerial shot that they took as of ten minutes ago. At that time, of the twenty-eight that are missing, seventeen of them are in this one area. By the time we land, those first ones should be out."

The picture that Thomas was looking at was marked by a large arrow. He could see that something was there, but to him it just looked like a blob.

You need to close your eyes and look at the front of the building. He told Linyah that he wasn't there. *But you have a photograph. Look at it and then close your eyes. I can help you find them.*

He did as she asked and when he closed his eyes, he could see what she meant. Not only could he see the building on the inside, but he also seemed to move along the corridors as well. He asked her how she was doing that.

I'm not, you are. I'm only showing you how to move. He saw a door and started to open it but looked on the other side. There was nothing there. Linyah laughed. *See, you're very good at this. Keep moving toward where you know the place is. You should be able to make your way through the debris without getting lost.*

He moved in and out of halls. He knew that the place that Misha was talking about was on the second floor, and when he found the staircase, he slowly opened the door and moved into the opening. Thomas felt someone touch his hand but didn't move. Moving up the stairs to the second floor, he paused. That's when someone spoke next to him.

"This is fucking amazing." Turning, he looked at Misha. "Nic told me to touch you but not to speak until I got where you are. Christ, this is going to be so helpful."

"Can you lead?" Misha shook his head. "Then you have to let me do this. No being the big brother, okay? Just let me lead us through this."

Misha nodded and Thomas reached beyond the door and could see the flames licking at the walls. He knew that whatever was going on in this reality couldn't hurt him, but it was a little disconcerting.

When you open the door, make a left, not a right. I know that the pictures say to go that way, but I think someone fucked the pictures up. He told Linyah he would. Once they cleared the doorway, he and Misha made their way to the door at the end of the hall. There were flames here as well, wires falling from the ceiling, as well as water flooding everything from the sprinklers. As they made it to the door, Misha told him to stop.

"This door. What's wrong with it?" Thomas looked at it. To him it looked like a smoke-stained door, a door like any other door they'd come across in situations like this. But then he looked closer. There was something...odd about it. Then it hit him.

It was blocked. There were chairs all up and down the hall, some of them turned over, others in front of doors too. But this chair had been put in front of it to keep whatever was inside where it was. They couldn't do anything about it at the moment, but Thomas looked into the room.

"They're all here." Misha nodded. "Someone wanted us to go the wrong way and not to find them when we figured it out. Whoever did this wanted them to die."

Your plane is landing. Nic and I are here now. Don't...under no circumstances are you to say anything about what you've seen. Misha asked Linyah why. *Because I have a feeling that whoever wanted this to go down this way is not going to take it well when you fuck up their plans. Nic and I will meet you in the building. Once we're there, we'll go the way the map told you. You and your brothers will rescue the people. I have a feeling that they're going to be watching to see that you go the way they want you to.*

As they were taken to the still burning building, things were not like they had expected them to be. The firemen were to stand down until they arrived and were hosing down the building even as they approached. It was a mess, and Misha said so.

Thomas just tried his best to not look at everyone as a murderer. As they geared up to enter, he reached for Linyah again and she told him she was on the second floor where he'd come out of the stairs. As they made their way up, Misha leading the way, Thomas asked Linyah if she was all right.

Yes. I've never slept so well in my life. He wanted to ask her about the note but was afraid to. But she answered his unspoken question before he could move on to something else. *I don't know what to say to you about loving me. I've never been in love before. I like you…very much, but I don't know if I love you. Is that all right?*

He could live with that and told her so. *I do love you. I never thought…I simply love you, and if you like me, then we can work with that. I want this to work. More than anything, I want this to work for us.*

I do as well. She laughed. *Now pay attention to what you're doing. I'm not going to have time to save your ass and get these people out too.*

Misha went through the door first and then him. Nic and Linyah were standing against the far wall, but when he moved toward her, she put up her hand and pointed to the camera. Nodding once, they started toward the right and Linyah and Nic seemingly blended in with them. At the next doorway, they all moved inside, appearing to check the rooms. As they entered, Nic told Thomas to take the hand of Carter and Phillip, and Nic held onto Misha and Andrew. In seconds, they were near the blocked door. Rider was staying behind so that it would look like they had split in half to check rooms. It was a great plan, and Misha said as much as they moved to the door.

The door was just as they'd seen it. Kicking the chair out of the way, Misha put his hand on the door to check for heat. The door was cool apparently as Misha kicked it in, having tried the lock and found it jammed. In seconds they were all in the room with the people they'd been asked to save.

Getting them out of the building was harder than coming in. The staircase was now burning and the other exit, the one closest to the front of the building, had been sealed shut with steel bars. Thomas handed the first woman a mask so she could breathe into his as he reached for Linyah. He explained what had happened.

We're having the same issues here. But you'll be happy to know that the men who are responsible for this are with us too. Rider and I found them and their nice little set up with the cameras. Nic is making sure that you find them as you're leaving. He laughed. *You should see these idiots. And their reason for doing this? Fucking stupid.*

He laughed again, relief that this was nearly over making him feel fantastic. The seriousness of the situation notwithstanding, he was happy she was there. But they still had to get out of there. Turning to the people they had found, a woman told him that she snuck out of the building several times a day to smoke and had found a quicker way out. As they moved toward the middle of the building, Thomas told Linyah what they were doing.

We'll meet you there. I don't have a problem with these idiots figuring out we popped them there. No one will believe them anyway after they tell them what they were doing here. Some people should be stood in front of a firing squad and shot. Several times. He told her he agreed with her and that they'd meet there. And within five minutes, they were on their way out of the collapsing building.

Misha stood in front of the fire marshal as well as three officers an hour later. Arson was the cause, of course, and when he pulled Rider forward to tell them what he'd found, he explained to them about the three men.

"Their plan, for lack of a better term, was to protect their cameras against heat and water damage. As the manager of this facility had told them repeatedly they did not work in that industry, that they'd have to seek other employment, they decided to kill them off to prove a point. They wanted people to know that if they had better working cameras, finding victims would be much easier. Lucky for us, we turned the opposite way when we got turned around up there." The fire marshal looked at the men, then back at Rider as if he too was having a hard time believing anyone could be that stupid. "They confessed. I have it on one of their cameras. When we walked in, they were putting their results on a website that had a few hundred thousand people watching. It's all there."

Handing over the DVD, Rider walked away. As he headed toward Thomas, Linyah walked up to stand next to him. His smile, the one that said to Thomas "I'm going to beat the living shit out of you" had him standing in front of Linyah. She laughed but didn't move. He was going to protect her even at the cost of bloodying his brother's nose.

"Boy oh boy, are you going to love me. I've talked to Misha. A lot. We'd like to offer you a job to work with us. Not behind the scenes, as you did this time, but right up front." Linyah looked at him, and he nodded. "You'll be a great asset to the team. And if you're with us, Thomas can get laid more often. He's much more relaxed with you around. I like to think of that as a perk for us all. Him being less tense, I mean."

A low growl slipped from Thomas's mouth, and Rider laughed. As he walked away after telling Linyah to think about it, Thomas pulled Linyah into his arms. She wrapped her arms around him, and he felt at peace once again.

"I can tell him no." Thomas laughed and told her good luck with that. "I would love to help you. It will keep me from messing up your house so much."

"It's our house, and I suddenly don't care what you do to mess it up. We'll just hire someone to follow you around to pick up after you." He kissed the top of her head. "Let's go home and make a bigger mess of our bed."

She grinned up at him and they were instantly standing in their room. Kissing her deeply, Thomas held her to him. He was in love, in love with the one person in the world that he'd never have picked for himself. Thomas was very glad that the fates, or whatever they were, had stepped in and showed him what a mate could do for you.

CHAPTER 10

Maribel was so excited. She'd been spending time with Sina and Kendra off and on over the last several days, but now she was going to have a girl's day out. Linyah was going to pick her and Hannah up in a few minutes, and she'd be having pizza and pop with a queen, a former queen, and a princess. She looked at her dress again, wondering if it was too formal for a lunch date.

Hannah was running late. Morning sickness had the poor little thing running back and forth between the bathroom and kitchen. The tea had helped a great deal, but when she was upset, nothing helped. Nerves would do that to you when you already had a baby there. Being a grandmother was the most exciting thing she could think of right now.

When someone knocked at the door, she moved to get it before she thought that she shouldn't. She was pissed more than she was angry to find her ex-husband standing there.

"What do you want?" Andy stood there with his hands in his jacket pocket and glared at her. "You're not coming in, and if you try that crap on me again, I'm going to blow you full of holes. I'm in too good a mood to let you mess it up."

"Where do you think you get off talking to me like that?" He lunged for her, but she pulled the gun that she'd been practicing with from her pocket. Linyah and Hannah had made sure she was ready for her ex-husband when he returned, and she was glad now that she'd taken the time to conceal it on her person. "You thinking of shooting me? What the hell is wrong with you? Go and get one of them boys and tell them to get you straightened out."

"I'm just fine and dandy, thanks. And I don't need straightening out. You might when I'm finished with you." She held the gun steady, something that Hannah had told her a million times. "You were told to get away from here or we'd call the police."

When he looked over her shoulder, she knew that she was no longer alone. Maribel was somewhat disappointed, as she'd wanted to deal with Andy on her own. When she turned slightly to look, she was surprised to see not only Hannah but Linyah as well.

"Watch him." She turned around when Linyah spoke and watched Andy. "We're just here for backup. Or a witness in the event you need one when you kill him. I'm hoping for the latter myself, but then I've dealt with his prick ass before. He's on my shit list. And heading to the top of it too."

"She ain't got it in her to kill me. And she can't either. I'm her mate." Andy looked at her. Then he smiled. She knew that smile. It was the one he'd used right before he slapped her around. Well, not this time. She watched him carefully now and tried not to get scared when he moved a step toward her.

"I'm gonna come in the house now." He reached for the handle and pulled the screen door open. "You just back on up and we'll talk. Just talk. Tell them girls to—"

She had no idea that she'd pulled the trigger until the wood on the floor right in front of Andy jumped up and cut into his face. He fell backwards, but he wasn't staying down. When the door tore from the hinges, he was stopped by Misha, and his cat did not look happy to see him any more than she'd been. But he only growled at his father and didn't lunge at his throat like she would have done as a cat.

"I've got this." Misha turned and looked at her. "I got this. You go on back with them girls. He's not going to touch me again. I swear to you, this is not going to end the way he thinks it's going to."

"You're going to pay for this." Misha moved to sit beside her and yawned hugely as Andy stood there screaming obscenities at her. "Motherfucking cunt. You put that fucking gun down and come on out here. I got me a thing or two to show you about respect for your mate. And I plan on showing that son of mine a thing or two when I'm finished too."

Linyah laughed. And then Hannah did. Misha never moved from his position on the floor, but Maribel did wonder if he was finding it funny as well. Respect? How the hell did you respect someone like her ex-husband when he'd never given any to them? Or for that matter, even to himself over the years.

"I'm not telling you again to get away from here. The next time I fire this thing, I'm going to hit you in the brain. And I'm talking about the only one you ever thought with." She lowered the gun until it was pointed at his dick. "The only good that thing did me was these boys.

And now I've got me a grandbaby on the way and more daughters coming in all the time."

"Daughters? You had daughters too? Christ almighty woman, what the hell did you go and make daughters for?" He looked over her shoulder again, and she wondered which one of the girls he was looking at. Maribel considered both of them her children already and would protect them with her life. "That big one there, the tall drink of water, she mine? She don't look too much like me. The other one is sort of scrawny if you ask me."

"No fucking way would I be one of your daughters. Christ." Linyah shuddered. "If I were a child of yours, you'd have been castrated, skinned, and hung out to dry before you got that tiny thing out to make another child. I can understand having respect for your parents, but you're not worth a pile of shit. As for the scrawny one, as you called her, she's more a leader than you ever dreamed of being."

He started forward again, but looked at her this time. Maribel wasn't sure she could really kill him, but she knew, she absolutely knew, that she could hurt him a great deal so that he'd wish he was dead. There was no way in hell that he was going to harm her again or one of her children.

"All right then, if you want to play this way. I'll just come out and tell you why I'm here. I want me a cut of the money them boys have been making. I'm their sire, and I think I deserve a cut. I'm thinking half. Without me, they'd not have shit." He looked at Misha, then back at her. "You tell' em. You tell' em that they're gonna pay me for siring them or so help me, I'll come back here when I know you're alone and tear you apart."

"You greedy bastard." Before she could tell Hannah not to get too close, she slapped Andy in the face. Maribel was so stunned by the action she could only stare. Misha stood up, but he never moved to attack. When his dad moved, it was all Maribel could do not to shoot. But she was terrified of hitting Hannah. She shouldn't have worried. Hannah had it well under control.

As soon as Andy reached for her, Hannah dodged. As he fell forward from the momentum, she turned and kicked him in the ass. Andy fell onto the floor, and Hannah leapt onto his back and slammed his head forward. No one moved, no one said a word as she hit him twice more before lifting his head up and turning him to see her.

"You are worthless. How you ever sired six of the most wonderful sons is beyond me. Hopefully our children won't be a thing like you. Why, to think that...you have no idea what sort of children you have, only seeing what they can give you. Isn't that right?" She hit his head again, and blood poured from his nose as she continued. "I'm going to let you up. Why I don't let Maribel...Mom shoot you right now, I have no clue, but you're going to get up, get out of our home, and never return. Because if you do, I'm going to hurt you worse than this."

Her cat took her. She was sitting atop him as a pretty little thing, then shifted to a wonderfully beautiful leopard in seconds. Her claw, sharp and huge, raked across his face to the bone. Blood not only poured from the fresh wounds but spilled on the floor into a large puddle. When she got off him, she flipped him over and dug her nails deep into his chest, almost like she was going to tear his heart out. It was Linyah who walked up to her and stopped her by putting her hand over her paw.

"I'm to understand that these wounds made by a leap leader will not heal. Right, Maribel?" She told her yes. Linyah nodded as she looked back at Hannah. "If you tear out his heart, if he even has one, the only thing you'll do is quicken his demise. Let him up. And every time he looks in the mirror he's going to know that to fuck with you is going to hurt. I personally would kill him, but you will do better by making him suffer as he's done to this family for years. Don't you think?"

Hannah didn't move. Misha moved to stand next to Hannah, but he didn't touch her. Maribel thought about putting her gun away because she knew there was no way she'd fire it now. If she did, she'd hurt one of her family, and she wasn't going to chance that. But she held it up, aimed at Andy. If he fucked up, she was going to kill him.

Hannah moved back, and so did Linyah. Misha moved to his mate, but he was careful to keep his eyes on his father. But when Andy stood up, he lunged at Linyah. Maribel never thought, never considered what she was about to do and fired twice. Andy Lanning dropped to the floor like the dead weight he'd always been.

~~~

Thomas watched his father's body being taken out. The police had been there for five minutes before he'd been able to get to the house. The frantic call from Misha had him dropping everything and racing to the house. And now all of his family was there, including his new in-laws. Misha had asked if he could take Hannah up to their room as soon as Thomas had arrived, and the police had let him. She had thrown up twice and the police, the shifters anyway, knew she was pregnant.

156

"This man, he was your dad?" He shook his head at Nildale. "Oh, I'm sorry. I thought he was your father. I apologize."

"He wasn't our father, but he did help create us. It was his total contribution to our existence. My mom raised us and took care of us. He was simply the thing that gave us to her." Nildale nodded and looked around the room.

There were more police in this room than he'd seen on most missions they'd gone on. Jackson, the household cook, and Mike were handing out coffee and food like they were working for the Red Cross. Thomas noticed that not one of the cops said no. Linyah walked up beside him and he pulled her into his arms.

"I should like a word with you both when you have the time. It's not important...well, that's not entirely true. It's very important, but it can wait. For a bit." Nildale laughed. "I'm mucking this up, aren't I?"

"We can talk now. Linyah can't leave just yet, but I'm sure that Misha won't mind if we use his office." Nildale was shaking his head. "Would you like to do this at our house?"

"No. If you wouldn't mind, at my home. I know it's a great inconvenience and all, but it is important that we do this correctly." He looked at Linyah as he continued. "It's time he was brought into the family."

When she nodded, her dad walked away. Thomas looked at her, waiting for an explanation, but she only shook her head and said later.

As the cops began to exit and the ambulance moved out, his mother sat down on the couch. He was glad now that Linyah had taught her how to use a gun. It more than likely saved all of them from being seriously hurt. Especially their mom.

"That nice policeman talked to me before he left. He said that...he told me that I'm not being charged." They all sat around, and drinks and snacks were brought to the big living room. "It was self-defense and I'm not going to be charged with anything. I guess when Hannah had me file that report the two other times he was here, someone had put out a restraining order."

Everyone looked at Rider. He smiled as he leaned back on the couch with his glass of tea.

"I had to do something. If it came to this, and I'm not saying I hoped it would, but we needed to have something that said he was a problem." Rider sat his glass of tea on the counter and took a plate overflowing with cookies. Thomas noticed that Linyah eyed them greedily but didn't take any. He thought he'd find out about that later. "I still want to know why on earth Hannah was covered in blood."

So did he. But his mom only shrugged and said nothing. Linyah too was being very quiet. And since Hannah wasn't in the room, it was hard to ask her. But they moved on to more important things. Like what to have for dinner.

"We're going out." His mom spoke up from the couch, then flushed. "I know that it seems strange now, but I've been looking forward to this luncheon thing all day. I'm not going to let some old poop head ruin it for me. If the girls are still willing, that is. But I think getting out of here is the right thing to do."

"I'm more than willing. I've been excited about having an all the way pizza since Nic told me what it was. And a soda. Do they call them sodas in this part of the country? Not that it matters, but I want a root beer." Sina stood up as she continued with her plans. "Also, I'd like to have a cherry turnover. I've no idea what they are but I want one. And I know that Kendra would be ready to go as well. She is so excited to try something new. Linyah? Do you think you can tear yourself from your male to go with us?"

"Yes. I'm ready when you are." Misha and Hannah entered the room just as they were trying to figure out how to go and ask Hannah if she wanted to go. Thomas laughed when she nearly knocked Misha down to get ready. As the women left, Linyah pulled him aside to speak to him.

"My father...you might want to talk to him before tomorrow." He nodded, and she kissed him on the mouth with a quick peck. Thomas pulled her back and deepened the kiss until they were both breathless. She was out the door before he could ask her why he needed to talk to her dad.

As they were seated in the living room again, Misha told them what happened. Not the version that they'd given the police, but what had really gone down. The police thought he'd come into the house and hurt Hannah, and his mom had defended her. The claw marks, all made by Hannah's cat, were explained away by Maribel by saying he'd had them when he got there. Where on earth, she'd asked the first officer, would she have gotten something to hurt him like that? Thomas was quite proud of his family all in all. They'd seen a problem and fixed it. It was a shame that someone had to die over it, but his father had never been much of a man, and he'd nearly hurt his mate. Thomas might have ended up killing him anyway if he wasn't already dead.

It worked, of course, with a little help from Linyah and her magic. She'd made it all look like it was a simple case of protecting their own. The blood, all of it except what was from the gunshot wound, was gone, as were the splinters in the floor from when his mom had shot at him the first time. But the police were satisfied with the story, and that really was all that mattered. Additionally, they no longer had to worry about Andrew Lanning lurking about every corner ever again.

Rider got up to answer his phone and returned almost immediately. He didn't look all that happy, and Thomas stood up to get ready to go out again. But he sat down, and the rest of them watched Rider as carefully as he did. Thomas wasn't sure how much more he could take today.

"Hannah's grandparents are on their way here. I have a buddy of mine watching them and as of ten minutes ago, they boarded a plane for here. They have hotel reservations at the hotel downtown for one night. They have also put in a flight plan for their trip home and included one more person...a Hannah Little." Misha said nothing, but Thomas could see his mind working as Rider continued. "I have sent a message to Linyah to let her know to watch; not that I think they'll suddenly appear, but maybe she can prepare Hannah for them."

"She'll be just fine." Thomas thought so too, but he was glad to hear Misha say it. "After today, I'd not want to fuck with her. She needed this. I never...when we got upstairs I thought for sure she was going to fall apart, but she was giddy. Not for hurting him, but because she'd stood up to him. I think we have Linyah to thank for that."

Thomas nodded. She'd been encouraging both Hannah and their mom for weeks now on how strong they were. Even Kendra, who one would think was strong, was listening to her little sister about matters of court. Thomas started to ask what Nildale wanted, but Misha spoke again.

"We're not going to stress over this. He'll try to take her or make her do something she doesn't want and she'll rip his throat out." Everyone laughed but Misha. "She's a good deal stronger than she was a month ago, and even stronger today than she was this morning. She'll be just fine. I, for one, am not worried about my mate. In fact, I think I'm more concerned with how this guy is going to react when she tells him to fuck off."

Thomas thought he was right. After talking a little more, he finally cornered Nildale. The man was laughing at something that Carter was telling him, and Thomas waited. He knew whatever it was, he'd give the man. He was in love with his daughter and had him to thank for that, in a small sort of way. When Carter left them, Thomas finally asked him what he needed.

"Linyah is a princess. You know that, right?" Thomas nodded, not sure where this was going. "You're a prince." Thomas waited for the punch line. Something that would make this a joke. But the longer he stood there staring at him, the more Thomas realized he wasn't kidding.

"No. No. That can't be right." Nildale nodded. "I'm just her male, her mate. Not a prince. She's...she's a princess, yes, and always will be, but I'm only her mate. She never said anything about me being a prince of anything."

"I'm sorry, son, but you are a prince." Thomas was still shaking his head when Nildale had him sit down. "You'll have duties, as you know. Not all of them are as boring as some. But you'll have your fair share of those too. There is a ball coming up, but that's—"

"I can't be a prince. I'm a leopard." Nildale leaned back in the chair and watched him. Thomas felt slightly stupid. "I'm a leopard, a member of the Lanning Search and Rescue team. I'm mate to Linyah Lanning and brother to the leader of our leap. I'm so not prince material. I'm controlling and never on time for things. I have things in my life that I'm not terribly proud of and things that I am."

"Yet here you are, mated to a princess, which has made you a prince." Nildale laughed. "I think you're going to be a fine prince. Once we get you in that wig and pantyhose. Oh, and the heels that we have to have you fitted for. They're a bitch to learn how to walk in, but you can get it sooner rather than later. What do you think of raw oysters? They have to be eaten before every dinner. Just to keep you in line with the rest of us."

Thomas stood up and then sat twice before he realized that Nildale was making fun of him. He growled low and waited another five minutes for the man to stop laughing. He was still wiping at his face when Thomas finally had enough.

"You are so not funny." Nildale laughed again, and Thomas leaned back in his seat. "You had me going there for a minute. I thought for sure you were going to tell me that I was going to be crowned and some sort of ceremony was going to take place."

Nildale said nothing, and Thomas felt a finger of fear run along his spine. He waited and waited for him to tell him that too was a joke. Needed him to tell him it was all a big prank against him. But he only snapped his fingers, and a small round crown was in his fingers. Thomas only stared at it.

"It's not like the king's that will grace the family someday when Kendra takes a male. His will be...well, bigger. Yours is much smaller and has less diamonds in it. The ceremony is simply a large gathering. No one is expected to bring you homage or anything like they would for a king, but there will be hundreds of guests." Thomas could only stare at the crown and barely heard what Nildale was saying. "I'd like to get this finished soon. The people will want to meet you. I'd expect a few of them to hit you up for some kind of favor."

"You're not kidding at all, are you?" Nildale shook his head. "I'm really a prince. I'm...I'm going to be wearing that thing and people are going to...what are people going to expect me to do? Christ, my brothers are going to love this."

"They'll be very proud of you, I think. And well, for starters, they won't take too kindly to you calling it a thing. It's a crown. And you must stop telling me this is a joke. It's not." Nildale handed him the crown, and Thomas stared at it. "You might as well take it to see how it feels. Sooner or later I'm going to set it on your head."

"Will my family be there?" Nildale nodded. "Can they not be? I mean, this is going to really give them a great deal to make fun of me about. Not that they don't have plenty right now. They think I'm a nerd. And for the most part I think I am as well, but this? This is going to make me a laughing stock in their eyes. So if you could, I'd rather they didn't see me fall on my ass and have to go chasing this thing down."

"I staple it to your head." Thomas looked at him sharply, and Nildale burst out laughing. "You really are too much fun, aren't you? No, I don't staple it to your poor head. But you'll be fine. I promise. Once you're crowned you'll be known as Lord Thomas and Linyah Lady Linyah. People will hit you up for favors as I've mentioned before. But nothing horrendous, I think. They'll be things like making so and so the overseer of this land or that. I take care of that part. Then there will be the women. They'll be all over you. But I'm pretty sure Linyah will take care that it doesn't go too far."

Thomas nodded. He was going to fuck this up. He just knew it. As he reached for Linyah to tell her what was going on, Nic sat down with his dad. His smile made Thomas think that something else was going on with this whole crowning thing and he was going to hate this even more.

"You have to wear a robe and carry a scepter too." Thomas didn't even look at Nildale for him to confirm or deny this. He was frankly too afraid to. "And then there's the ring you have to kiss. It will be on my finger at the time and you'll pay homage to me."

"You're full of shit." Both Nildale and Nic started laughing. Thomas watched them for several minutes, wondering what the hell was wrong with them, when he smiled. He was going to get them back if it was the last thing he did. As they continued to laugh he got up and left them there, leaving the crown on the table where Nildale had put it. There wasn't any such thing going to happen; he'd been played all along. He just knew it.

Misha was on the phone when he found him in his office. As he hung up, Thomas asked him if things were okay. He nodded and stared out the window beside his desk for a long time before he spoke.

"I've just spoken to my lawyer. I'm being sued for kidnapping Hannah. And if I give her up, convince her to go with her grandparents, the suit will be dropped."

Thomas didn't know what to say. "I'm not going to, but I do plan to tell her what's going on. But I know...she'll think I should do it. I know that she will."

"I don't know. She loves you a great deal and is excited to be having your baby." Misha nodded but said nothing. "These people, do we know when they're going to arrive?"

"In the morning." Thomas nodded this time. "I have to talk to the family about this. I know that the women are out having fun, so we'll get together when they get back. If I had more time...if we had more time, I'd say let them have until later. But we can't. I was wondering if you could let Linyah know. Maybe she can prepare Hannah for this."

He said he would and reached for his mate. She sounded so full of life that he hated to take that away from her. But when he told her what was going on, she told him she had it covered. She told him that over the last several days, she and Hannah had worked out a brilliant plan to make these people leave them the hell alone.

We're going to make him wish he'd never heard of the Lanning Leap. Hannah and I have been planning this for days now, and she's so excited to be standing up to someone. After today, who knows how this will turn out? But she'll be just fine. He asked her what she was going to do. *Never mind. You just let us take care of it. Hannah needs this more than she thinks she does, and telling her grandparents off is going to make her confidence level shoot through the roof.*

He told Misha, who smiled before speaking. "Do you think we can have a part in all this? I need something too."

Tell him that everyone has a part and his is the best. Thomas wasn't sure if this was a good idea, but to see his brother smiling like he'd just been awarded a big check was going to make it worth it. Even if he had to sell his house to bail them all out.

CHAPTER 11

Howard Little watched the tiny little thing bring his wife a wine. He was going to fire her as soon as they landed. There was no point in doing so now because he'd just have to listen to her whine about not being employed. But he'd told the staff a million times that his wife was to get nothing unless he said it was okay. Damned bitch would learn her place or she'd just have to suffer the consequences. Carole looked at him before she took a sip. And she was going to learn her place as well. He didn't like this new her. She was acting like a child and it had all started when she'd found out that her granddaughter was still alive.

"You've been getting very uppity here lately." His wife of forty-seven years said nothing as she took the small plate of vegetables too. "Did I tell you that you could ruin your meal with snacks? What are you trying to do, Carole, piss me off before we even land?"

He reached for the plate only to have her jerk it from his reach. Howard was so shocked he could only stare at her. But when she sat it with the wine glass on the small table, he started to rise. This was going just too far and it was time to put her back into the place he liked her in.

"Touch me and I will side with Hannah about coming to live with us." Howard had no idea who she thought she was talking to, but he slapped her before she said another word. Everyone cleared out of the room until it was just the two of them. He watched her as the blood from her lip swelled, then spilled down her chin. She made no effort whatsoever to clean it up, and that pissed him off more.

"I've had enough of this shit from you. Do you hear me? You'll behave yourself or I will make sure you regret it for a long time. I will not have insolence from you. Where are you getting this idea that you can do as you please? Since your son left us, you've been acting out. Well, I won't have it." She didn't say a word nor did she wipe the blood from her lip. "Get cleaned up. You sicken me."

Carole stood up, but when she staggered slightly, he waited for her to fall. He loved it when she fell. It was his perfect chance to tower over her. She'd fall, and he'd stand over her without touching her as she struggled to stand up. But this time she only held onto the back of her chair as she steadied herself. Damn it all to hell. Nothing was going the way he'd planned it, and he was going to figure out where he'd lost control. And soon too. He could not, would not have people thinking he was weak ever again.

When she was gone, he felt his anger toward all of this tomfoolery come to a head again. To have to take time out of his busy work day to retrieve his granddaughter was simply too much. She should learn her place too or he'd show her the consequences as he'd done to her mother. And that had not worked out so well either. He thought— well, he'd hoped—that she'd get out on her own and realize that she couldn't do it. Not without her daddy's money. But she'd been killed and his granddaughter had been taken. If that wasn't bad enough, now she had resurfaced and he had to fix that too. She would do as he told her. If her mother had done what he'd said, she'd be here and he'd not be flying nearly across the United States to clean up her mess. Howard called for his secretary, who came out of the back part of the plane almost immediately. She had her pen and pad out to do whatever it was he told her. Just as things should be.

"Get a message to that Lanning person, Misha I believe his name is. Tell him that I want to meet my granddaughter as soon as we land. She will come to my hotel and we'll have a nice talk. Tell him his company is not welcome or needed. I will have this taken care of today and not later. I need to return home as soon as possible." Carla nodded as she wrote out notes. "And whatever kind of name Hannah is, I want you to file something to have it changed back. Her mother's name will do nicely. She no longer has any use for it so that will work. Kelli is a ridiculous name but for now, until I can pawn her off in some business dealings, it will have to do."

He had never particularly cared for the name Kelli, but it was the principle of the thing now. He should have been there to name his daughter, and since he had been at a conference when she'd been born, he'd had no say in it. Well, he'd take care of it now. His wife had paid dearly for that mistake if he remembered correctly. There were other things he needed Carla to do as well.

"Cut off my wife's spending. All of it. And she is to have a maid that will listen to me sit outside her door at all times. If she leaves the room, I want to know about it. If she makes a call...you know what? Have her cell phone cut off as well. There is no reason for her to have it anyway. She has no friends that I don't approve of, and they only talk to me when they want something from her." Carla said she would take care of it, and Howard had a thought. "My granddaughter...what else have you found out about her and that family she is living with? Any news on getting their marriage dissolved?"

"No sir, not yet. They have been married for a few months now, and we must make sure that there is no child." Howard would take care of it himself if there happened to be one. "And then there is the money. She has a great deal of it at her disposal. If she needed to, I do believe she'd be able to hire herself a good lawyer. I do not foresee her going against you, but with these younger people, who is to say what stupidity they will do?"

"I know that this Lanning person has given her whatever she wants, the fool. But her money is not a problem to me. I didn't even look into his finances. He does not make enough to make a difference to me." He'd cut that out as well, her having her own accounts. That was something that Howard prided himself on. If he didn't like it, or it didn't work, he'd simply cut it out. It was why he had the nickname of "little chopping block." And he loved it.

After making sure that she had a list enough to make this work, he settled back in his chair. His wife came out of the bathroom and sat down in her seat just as her wine and plate was taken away. She only smiled at him and he wanted to hit her again. But the pilot said they would be landing soon and he didn't want her a mess again. But she'd pay.

Since Daniel had come to this godforsaken land and talked to his granddaughter, Carole had been acting a little out of sorts. Then when Daniel announced that he was moving, she started disobeying him at every turn. It had started out small, almost unnoticeable at first. Then she'd gotten mouthy with him a little too often. Howard had taken to locking her in her room during the day when he'd have to go to the office. It was a damn nuisance.

Then there was Wanda. Smiling, he thought of how he'd gotten her to play along. He'd tried to get Daniel to give up on the woman when he'd announced he was in love, but when he figured he could use her addiction, he let the courtship and marriage go as planned. He'd even given them a house to live in, one he had set up with cameras all over the house so he could keep tabs on them. Then this thing with his granddaughter gave him the prime time to bring Wanda back into her sickness and get two things at once. Wanda would give him the grandchild he didn't want in Kelli's child, and he'd have her committed because of her gambling. It was perfect.

Until recently.

Wanda had called him just last week. "I can't make her do what you want. She said that she's in love with her husband and that...and that she won't leave him. I think she's a good deal stronger than you think."

"Stronger than me? I think not. You get her to come here or so help me, I'll tell Daniel what you've done and make sure that every club you've joined knows what sort of sick person you are." She didn't say anything, which surprised him. Normally she would beg him or even sob a little, like that was going to change his mind. "You hear me? I will ruin you."

"You already have." The phone went dead, and it was everything he could do not to call her back and demand that she hang up the phone properly. Instead he called in a few favors. He may not live near them any longer, but money spoke volumes when you wanted something done. He was wondering how many times she'd been arrested now. The man he spoke to said he'd take care of everything. Howard had expected reports but wasn't concerned about them right now. He'd get a full rundown when he landed. But then things there were not as he'd planned either. Not really. He'd hoped that she'd call back, beg him to back off. But he never heard from any of them.

Howard had tried to call her several more times over the next few days. She never answered. His calls were directed right to voicemail. He had left her a few messages at first, stern ones telling her all the things he was going to do to her when he got her back home. It never occurred to him that his son wouldn't come back to the fold. When Howard wanted something, he damned well got it. He was tempted to call his son, and finally after several more days of nothing, he gave in. But Daniel too had his calls redirected. It was the reason he was flying out here. It was time to jerk them back to his part of the civilized world. It was hard enough controlling them when they lived close. But when they were this far away, it was more difficult.

As soon as the plane touched the ground, he was barking orders. There was a limit to how much time he'd spend in this area, and the sooner things got finished, the sooner he'd get back to his well-ordered life. The first thing he did was fire the waitress. As he waited at the door for the stairs to disembark to be put in place, he reached for Carole's hand and squeezed it as tightly as he could without breaking bones.

"You fuck around anymore and you'll regret it. Do I make myself very clear to the empty fucking head of yours?" She nodded but didn't give him what he wanted.

When he took her to her knees by squeezing tighter, she whimpered. Howard let her go. "When we return home, you're going to have to learn your place again. And until that time, you will be confined to your room."

Straightening his tie, he pasted his meet-and-greet smile on his face and reached for Carole. Her hesitation had him smile inwardly, but she finally gave it to him. His appearance to the world was important to him, and she was a part of his well-crafted image.

The limo was right where he wanted it. There was a man standing there, just as he liked, with the full uniform of his kind…hat, white gloves, and tux. It was as it should be. As they slid into the car, he reached for his phone and called Carla.

"Have the room set up the way I asked, luncheon for three only in the biggest private room this hotel has. The plane will be ready to go at a moment's notice, and I don't want to have to wait until the locks are in place before we can leave with my granddaughter. You have put in an order for a cage put in the back room, haven't you?" She said it was being done now. "Good. See that she is cleaned up as well. There is no telling what sort of germs she might have gotten from these people. And I need a doctor onboard. If there are…complications, I want them taken care of now."

As soon as he hung up, he looked at Carole. She'd been the instrument to him getting to this point in his life, but he was sick of her. She would have to be put away soon too. He needed his freedom. More than that, he wanted to be able to come and go as he pleased without her as a burden. Frist thing he was going to do when he got home again was call his lawyer. And the sympathy that her being "ill" would bring him would be good as well.

"Do you really think it's going to be so easy?" He looked at her, wondering if he should slap her again for speaking without permission. "I hope she's more like Kelli than you think. Her defying you was the best thing that ever happened to her."

"And she was murdered because she defied me." She only smiled at him. "You're becoming somewhat of a troublesome thing that I'm sick of. Do you remember what happens to you when you get it in your head that you can do as you please? Do you really think that I'm going to let this go on much longer? I'm not, in the event you haven't figured that out yet."

"I don't really care what you want or don't want any longer." She smiled bigger, and he had a second, just a split second, of fear. "But I've been busy too, you should know. Busy getting things the way that I want them. And if this turns out the way I hope, you'll be the one who is hurting."

He hit her. His fist was out so quickly and connected with her so soundly that he surprised himself. As she lay slumped over in the seat, he tried to think what to do now. There was no way he'd be able to get her into the hotel without people seeing what a mess she was. Pressing the button that slid the glass down just enough so that he could speak without him seeing the mess his wife had made, he told the driver to go past the Lanning offices. He wanted to see what kind of person this man was. Not that he was worried.

The drive proved to be just enough. Carole woke, but she looked at him differently. The smile, no matter how many times he insulted her or threatened her, would not leave her face. And the blood on her blouse was too glaring for his taste too. She was going to make him take matters into his own hands, and he was actually looking forward to it.

"Clean up." She only sat there. "I swear to Christ, when we get this nasty business over with, you are going to pay for this."

Still nothing. Howard was getting sick to death of this. He was going to lay down the law and have things put back to order. First thing was bringing the girl home. Then he was going to bring his son home as well. That wife of his was finished too, as well as his own. Things were going to be just as he wanted them in very short order or hell would be paid.

~~~

Hannah paced back and forth. Daniel and Wanda were sitting on the couch as if they were expecting some gun men to come in and kill them both. Linyah only watched and waited. Hannah was going to do fine, and the rest of the family would as well. Smiling, Linyah looked over at Maribel.

"What time to we need to leave here?" She knew but was trying to make sure that everyone was less tense. "And have you heard from the men yet?"

"Misha said that everything is in place. And we need to leave here in about ten minutes. Are you sure this is going to be okay?" They both looked at Hannah, who was pale and had been sick several times since they'd all arrived at her home about an hour ago.

"Everything will be just fine. Mr. Little thinks that he is very powerful, but things are not always as they seem." That was for sure. Her mom and dad appeared in the room just as Jackson came in to say the car was ready. Hannah looked ready to run.

"I can help you." She nodded, and Linyah touched her belly. She only took the sickness away and bathed the baby in security. The smile that Hannah gave her made her smile as well. "You're going to kick his ass, you know that, right? This man is not going to know what hit him."

"I am." She didn't sound very confident, but that was okay. Hannah would be great. "I'm glad you're here. I don't tell you that enough, but I'm very glad you and Thomas found each other."

She was as well. And this morning while he was deep inside of her, roaring out his release, she'd told him she loved him. Thomas told her several times that when this thing with the Littles was over, he was going to tie her to their bed and eat her everywhere. She was looking forward to that.

As they rode to the hotel, she thought about her conversation with Carole Little. Linyah had visited her several times over the past few days. The woman had been so...beaten that Linyah had promised her that she'd help her as well. Linyah had to fight hard not to find Howard every time she thought of Carole's face when she'd simply popped into her bedroom. He had used her as a punching bag more times than Carole could remember.

"You get caught here and he'll tear you apart. Run now before...how did you get in here?" Linyah told her that she was magical, and Carole had only nodded. "Do you have any magical food on you? I've not eaten for five days."

Leaving her and returning seconds later with several bags of food, she watched as the woman ate like she was afraid she'd never have another meal. While she had her fill, Linyah looked around the room. It was the most depressing thing she'd ever seen.

There was a bed, a cot really, that was as bare as the walls. A single blanket without a pillow lay on the neat, smallish sheet. There was no dresser in the room and her clothing, what little there was, had been folded neatly and put on the floor in nice piles. A towel hung over the shower curtain bar in the bathroom. There was a toilet in the room but the mirror and towel rack had been removed. Rugs, curtains, and other things to make the room look like something other than a prison were missing as well. Carole looked around the room when she asked her about it.

"I'm so used to it now that I rarely see it. He takes things from me, things he thinks I like as punishment. It matters little what he thinks I've done wrong, but there you have it." Carole thanked her politely for the food. "Could you tell me that you aren't a figment of my imagination?"

"I'm not. I'm sister-in-law to Hannah." She nodded and wiped at the tears. "Would you like to see her?"

"More than anything in the world, but not yet. Not here. Not like this." She looked around. "Her mother was killed. I miss...I wanted to help my daughter. I had a plan to help her, but I was too late in getting this done. I was going to send her away before Howard found out about the baby. But he'd found her vomiting in the toilet and took her to the doctor. I never saw her again after that. He tossed her away just like he does most things he hates."

"I thought your daughter had reconciled with him and was to return home that day she was murdered." Carole shook her head. "You mean that he was playing her? And you? If you don't mind telling me, I'd like to know what happened."

"Howard had been so kind to her on the phone when she'd gotten in touch with us. I was almost fooled by it myself. She'd called here, you see, and before I could catch the call, he'd gotten it. He was bringing her home in the event someone found out who she was is what he told me later. He was terrified that someone would associate her having a bastard with him, and he just couldn't have it. So he lied to her. Had me do the same." She looked at her, and Linyah had wanted to take her away then. "Can you bring me someone? A lawyer? I want to make some changes to…I want to take care of a few things."

"I can." She'd reached for Thomas, and he told her who to use. In minutes, Conrad Leonard was in the room with them, and he was making changes to Carole's will. The man, a wolf, was appalled at the conditions that she was living in. Two hours later, she took him back with a promise she'd visit Carole often. But she also made Linyah promise that she'd not tell anyone that she'd seen her.

So the plan was set, and Carole was going to be surprised by the events as much as her husband was going to be. Linyah looked at Wanda when she said her name.

"Daniel said to tell you thanks." Linyah nodded. "He also said to thank you for having me come to him. He said…he had guessed there was a problem and it was the deciding factor that had us moving here. I was…he said he loves me. And that made it all better. Not great but better. I'm getting help again."

"Of course he does." Hannah took her aunt's hand and held it. "You're going to be fine. You're going to those meetings, and Uncle Daniel is going with you. He does love you. And when Mr. Little is gone, we'll go on more shopping sprees."

"He's not going to like you calling him Mr. Little." Hannah smiled and Linyah had to laugh. Wanda laughed as well as she continued. "You're so much braver than I am. I can hardly call him anything, and you're going to defy him right off. This is going to be epic."

"It is, isn't it?" Hannah looked at Maribel. "I love you as well. I don't tell you that often enough, but I do. I'd like it if you let me call you Mom too. I know it's a big step and all, but — "

Maribel hugged her and laughed. "I've been wanting to hear you ask for days now. Oh, honey, I'm thrilled to death. I heard you call me that when Andy was at the house, and I could have wept with joy. And now you're doing it for real. I love you so much, child. So very much."

As the limo came to a smooth stop, Linyah reached into the hotel and found Carole. She'd been hurt. Linyah asked her if she wanted her to come and get her. Linyah would have too, gone up to the room and torn the man apart just to save the poor woman from any more abuse from him.

No. No. I'm going to be just fine. I'm looking forward to this, and every time he thinks he's putting me in my place, the better it's going to be for me. I heard from Leonard as well. He said that the house locks have been changed and that all the servants have been dismissed. That was a fine idea you had in getting rid of his employees. I don't know how you're keeping them from telling on me, but I do appreciate it.

It was no problem, and I've taken care of them for you until you decide what you want to do. Linyah had had them put into a nice deep sleep. None of them were harmed, of course, but they were in no position to let the cat out of the bag just yet. *Are you ready for this? Ready to meet your granddaughter?*

I'm not and I am. Linyah told her she understood. *That nice young man of yours, Thomas, has brought me some lunch. I know that we're meeting you all downstairs soon, but there will more than likely be no time for eating.*

Probably not. Thomas had helped her a great deal with this after she'd told him what was going on. He'd been furious about Howard's treatment of his wife and they had, together with his mom, set her up in a nice house not far from their own home. She could come and go as she pleased, but be able to visit when she wanted. Howard was no longer going to be a concern for her. For any of them if things went the way they'd planned.

The room had been set up for a large party instead of the small one that Howard had ordered. There were shifters all over the hotel in the event something went wrong. And the police had been notified that something might happen. Those, too, were shifters and understood what exactly they might be walking in on.

Tables were set in long rows with beautiful flowers at every third place setting. Water pitchers had been set up as well as tall glasses. Linyah thought it looked very festive. Quite a contrast to the mess that was more than likely going to go down.

They were there first, of course, and the men, all the brothers and Nic, along with her dad, were waiting for them. Each of the Lanning men were milling about as humans, but were ready to become a cat should the need arise. As soon as they entered the room and sat down, the wait staff began bringing in platters of small sandwiches as well as cold drinks. Linyah was almost too excited to eat. It wasn't until Thomas sat next to her and took her hand that she felt calmer.

"He's here. I saw him come in. Hannah looks a great deal like her grandmother." Linyah nodded and told him she thought so as well. "I've heard from Leonard too. He said not only has he filed the divorce papers for Carole, but he's also filed a restraining order. The board members of her company are going to be informed of the change in the morning."

"Several of them are planning to leave soon. I'm thinking that once Howard is gone, things will work out for everyone." Thomas kissed the back of her hand. "I love you."

"And I love you as well." He kissed her again, this time on the mouth. "When we are finished here, I'd very much like to find a dark quiet place and take you hard and fast. Then take you to our bed and fuck you again and again. Are you up for that?"

Her body responded, and she wanted to tell him now would be good. But he only laughed and told her later. She was going to have to make him pay for that.

The manager of the hotel came into the room and said that the Littles were on their way down. It was show time.

CHAPTER 12

Hannah wanted to run. She was terrified beyond belief that this man was going to hurt her. And not just her but her unborn child as well. Putting her hand over her still flat belly, she talked softly to him and told him how much she loved him.

"The man we meet today is going to be your great-grandfather. Not that I think you'll have much to do with him after this meeting, but you never know." Rubbing him again, she smiled. "I cannot wait to meet you."

Comforted now, she looked up when everyone stood up. She reached for Misha's hand and as soon as he touched her, she felt his love flow over her. Standing too, she looked at her grandparents as they both walked into the room. To say she was disappointed would have been an understatement. She wasn't even sure why she was, only that...well, he was nothing like she'd thought he'd be.

He was tall and skinny, not the big robust man she'd envisioned. His hair was dark, much too dark for a man his age at sixty-six, and she figured that vanity had played a big part in his appearance. He had a mustache that curled at the tips and his mouth, a hard, fine line right now, looked like he had nothing in the way of a smile. And when he did finally smile, she had a feeling it was as fake as he was. And not just a little sinister.

"I believe we've been taken to the wrong room. Sorry to have bothered you." The manager, who had brought them in, assured her grandfather that this was the right room. Mr. Little looked right at her and glared. "What's the meaning of all this? I ordered you to come alone and that we were to have a nice talk. I made arrangements for this room to have a meeting. I'm afraid you'll all need to leave except my granddaughter. I have important business to discuss with her, and you are not welcome any longer."

He even moved to the side as if he was expecting everyone to do as he'd said. But Misha sat down, followed by the rest of them. Mr. Little didn't look at all pleased. Clearing his throat, he tried again, this time looking at Uncle Daniel.

"I'm not sure what this is about, young man, but I suggest you do as I tell you and clear these people out. I've had just about enough of your insolence, and you will do as I say or so help me I will make you regret defying me." Again he moved, but no one moved, not even Uncle Daniel. At a nod from Linyah, Hannah stood up.

"Hello. You must be Howard and Carole Little. I'm Hannah Lanning. This is my family. My husband, Misha Lanning. This is his mother, Maribel Lanning—"

"I do not care who they are. I demand that you to get rid of them this minute. You will learn to not disobey me, Hannah. I've gone to great lengths to set this up, and I will not have my commands thwarted at this point." His voice was sharp, and she flinched from it. When he smiled at her, all Hannah could think of was Bella and her ability to hurt her when she found a weapon. "You'll do as you're told right now. I demand respect."

"You can demand all you want, but it's not going to happen the way you want it to. So no, I'm not going to toss them out. Now, as I was saying." Hannah took a deep breath before she continued. "This is my mother-in-law, Maribel Lanning. And her other sons, Rider, Carter, Thomas, and his soon-to-be-wife, Linyah. Next is—"

"Perhaps you didn't understand me. I said that I do not care who these people think they are to you. Get out." He crossed his arms over his chest and glared at her. But Hannah knew as surely as she stood there that if she backed up, even a tiny bit, he'd run right over her all the time.

"Listen here. I'm trying to be polite and you're getting on my last nerve. You are not to interrupt me again. I want you to meet my family. You, Mr. Little, are being rude. Now shut up and listen to me." She thought she heard someone laugh and couldn't be sure but she thought it was her grandmother. "Now, where was I? Oh yes. This is Andrew and Phillip. You know Uncle Daniel and his wife. But this is Linyah's parents, Nildale and Sina. Everyone, this is Howard and Carole Little. Parents to my deceased mother, Kelli Little."

"Are you quite finished?" She nodded and smiled at him. "Very well then. I'm very happy to meet you all. But this is a private matter and I've come a long way to talk to my granddaughter. I would be very glad if you all were to just leave."

"I'm afraid that's not going to happen." Misha stood up as he spoke. "This is my wife, and after asking her what she wanted, she said she wanted us to stay. Whatever you have to say to her, you can say to all of us.

So I'd like to get this started as well. Mrs. Little, would you like something to drink?"

"No, she does not want anything to drink. I will tell her when she is thirsty. Young man, I don't know who you think you're talking to, but you are messing with the wrong man here. I have bought and sold men like you every day before breakfast. Now, I've been polite up until now and I—"

"No, you haven't. You've been a bully and a bastard." Hannah watched her grandmother as she walked away from her husband and continued talking. "Yes, Misha, I'd love a drink. Some juice if you have some. And I'd very much like to have a seat next to Hannah."

"Get your ass back here." Mr. Little looked like he was going to explode, and Hannah thought it was funny. Her grandmother sat down next to her and kissed her cheek, then turned back to her blustering husband.

"I'm leaving you, Howard. Not good timing, I suppose, but with the help of this lovely young woman, I've filed for divorce, taken my home back, and have fired your entire staff. The spies you have watching me had no idea what kind of things I had going on right under your nose. Also, the board members have been given the option of staying or leaving. I hope that they'll leave, but then it's up to—"

"Divorce? On what grounds? And you cannot leave me. Don't be absurd. Get your ass over here right now and I'll not go too hard on you when you return to my home." Grandmother just laughed. "Carole, I'm sick of this. I've no patience for you acting out like this. It's bad enough that I have to deal with these people, but you are not going to get away with this. Come here and I'll forget the entire thing."

"Did you know that the house was still in my name? I had an attorney look into that for me. He said you did that so that if anything happened with my father's business they couldn't take that. And until that moment, I'd forgotten that the business was my father's, not yours. You have no rights to any of it after the divorce. It's in the pre-nup my smart father had you sign. The company too, I found out, is still in my name. Your name doesn't appear to be anywhere."

Mr. Little moved forward, and Thomas stepped in front of him. The anger boiling off the man was hot enough to cook things on. And Linyah thought it was funny. "Get out of my way."

"You touch her in any way other than a slight pat on the back for being so brave and I will rip your arm from the socket and shove it so far up your ass you'll need to open your mouth to wave." The threat—and there was no doubt that was what it was—was given low and with enough menace in Thomas's voice that her cat stirred along her skin. Mr. Little must have felt the power of his words as well because he took a step back.

"I came here to take my granddaughter back with me." Thomas nodded. "She will come with me now or I'll sue you all for kidnapping her. I've no problem calling my attorney right now and having him draw up the papers."

"And what do you plan to do with the babe she carries? What will people say when they find out you plan to drug her and have the baby aborted from her body? What do you suppose the board members will think when you have her locked in a room, a room much like the one that your wife has been staying in for all these years to keep her from embarrassing you again? As you believe her mother might have." Mr. Little glared at her and

Hannah lifted her chin. "Before you can do any of the things that are working through your mind right now, you're going to have to get by each of us. And I'll warn you now, it will not be an easy trip."

Hannah didn't have to look to see that Misha and the rest of them had shifted. She did glance at her grandmother, who had tightened her grip on her hand but didn't move. She knew then that Linyah had warned her. Looking at her sister Linyah, a short nod confirmed it. When Thomas stepped back from Mr. Little, Hannah stood up.

"My family and I will remain here. You may visit if you wish, but it will be monitored visits, with my family surrounding me. My baby will be loved, taken care of, and will be safe. Safe from monsters such as yourself. He'll have a much better life than the one that I had."

"Yet you learned nothing from Bella's treatment of you. You think now that you are away from her treatment of you that you'll be fine? Never. I'll see to that." The room was silent. Even the big cats that had taken a seat stood up. He'd known where she was all along. And he'd never done a thing to help her.

"Howard?" He looked at his wife, who looked like he'd hit her. "You knew we had a granddaughter? You knew that she was...you said you never could find out anything about her. You said that as far as you knew, Kelli was dead and that her child had died with her...you told me that you found the records. You knew? All this time, you knew?"

"Well, of course I did. So what? She'd still be missing to you too if this idiot hadn't gone to great lengths to find us. Bella was getting paid very well for keeping her out of the papers. It's not like I knew right away. Christ, I would have taken care of the child long before the likes of Bella Oliver found her. Kelli's child was almost five when I found out where she was. But I did watch over them. I made sure that there was no record of her that would attach her birth to us." Mr. Little looked at her. "You had a roof over your head, food in your belly, and things to wear. I made sure of that. So what if she knocked you around a bit? You're still alive, aren't you?"

"You monster." Sina stood up and punched her finger into his chest as she continued. "Do you have any idea what this child endured? What kind of horrors she had to go through, what she was treated like? My goodness, man, did you not have any compassion at all for your own granddaughter?"

"Granddaughter?" He laughed. "Granddaughter? She'd not even be here if not for the fact that no doctor would abort her by the time I found out. Christ, woman, do you have no idea what a bastard child can do to a man like me? A man with money and prestige will be treated like shit when it's found out that he has a bastard in the family. It's not pretty, let me tell you."

Uncle Daniel stood up and walked to his father. Mr. Little was smiling, but when his son spit in his face, he lifted his hand to no doubt slap him. But Linyah reached him first and pulled his hand behind his back and forced him to the floor.

"Little here has been a very busy man in the past several weeks since he's been blackmailing Wanda. And so you know, I've done my own little investigation, but mine was on a more personal level." Linyah looked at Hannah. "You have two more relatives. An uncle and an aunt. Not that he'll claim them, but they are his bastard children. Both of them have been sent away; their mothers, sadly, are dead. I'm not sure he had anything to do with that, but with him? I don't doubt it. I have information on them should you want to find them." Hannah nodded and smiled.

"You lie." Linyah pulled his arm tighter behind him when Mr. Little spoke. "You fucking cunt. You're going to regret this."

"Doubtful. I rarely regret anything I do." Nildale laughed and the room did as well. "He was going to have Hannah committed until such time as her name could be changed, which has been stopped. I've also taken the liberty of stopping that nice woman who works for you. The cage you had put on the plane to hold Hannah has been dismantled and is going to be sold for scrap. He thought you to be some animal that he was going to have put down if there were too many issues. And when I say put down, that's just what I mean."

"You really have fucked with the wrong family there, Little." Nildale laughed again. "Yes sir, this is not a family to mess with. And as for your supposed riches? They're gone as well. I helped Carole here invest in some very nice businesses, and you, my good man, are broke. Oh, and the off-shore account has been moved. Carole thought a nice home for young mothers to be would be a good use for that money. She's calling it Kelli's Home. Nice ring to it, don't you think?"

"You put it all back right now. My wife is not in her right mind. I've been sheltering her for years. It's depression, and she's...that money is mine." Mr. Little struggled against Linyah, who held him tighter. "Wait until you release me. I'm going to own your ass."

"No, that would belong to me." Thomas helped Mr. Little stand and then sat him hard in a chair. "Do you see the cats around the room? It occurred to me just now that you're not the least bit surprised by them. Not even a little freaked out. So I took a little walk around your head. My goodness, you are a sick son of a bitch, aren't you?"

"What do you mean, you searched my head? That's not possible. And so what if I know a few shifters? I'm a man of the world. A very wealthy and powerful man. You'd do well to remember that, young man." Thomas sat down. "I suppose this is the part where you tell me I'm going to leave here and never return."

"No, I could care less if you left or stayed, but you're going to leave everyone in this room alone." Little snorted. "There are some things I'm going to tell you, however. A man like you, seemingly obsessed with the need for more money, isn't going to walk away from this without a few consequences. A worthless prick like you should know — and this is so much fun for me — that all the other money you had hidden in that house of yours has been found and is going to be distributed to some very needy charities as well. But you want to know something really funny? You are by far the poorest man in this room, even before we stripped you clean of what you had. That man over there, my brother Misha, is worth just over twenty-five million dollars. My mother, just over fifteen million. She would have more, but she just invested in a few companies recently and hasn't seen the return yet. My brother Rider...he's very stingy with his money and has just under fifty million. The others have about twenty million each. Me? Now there's a different story altogether. I married into money."

"So you plan to live off your wife and her family? I can admire you for that. Perhaps we have more in common than you think." Thomas only laughed. "You think we're not cut from the same cloth?"

"I don't. And I have my own money, a great deal more than Rider. I'm more of a penny pincher than even Rider. Not counting my wife's money, I'm worth nearly a billion dollars. Her money, coming from a long line of kings and queens, is worth more than I can put zeros to." Thomas leaned back in his chair and winked at her before he spoke again to Mr. Little. "I now own a controlling interest in your wife's company. Not that she needed it, but she knew that Daniel would need some help, and since I'm going to be around for a long while, she thought I could help keep it running for her."

"It's mine." Thomas hit him in the face with his fist and his head snapped back. When Thomas stood up and turned to Hannah, she stood as well. Hannah walked to the still screaming man and sat down.

"I'd like to tell you something you might not get just yet. I'm Hannah Lanning. I'm going to have a baby. I will continue to live with my husband and my new family for as long as I have in this life. I'm going to help my grandmother in any way she wants, keep her safe, and make sure she knows how much I'm glad she's in my family." Mr. Little looked at her, and she could almost see his mind working. "You, sir, are no longer welcome here. Not in this state, not in my life."

When she stood up, she felt rather than heard him move. Her hand morphed as she turned, and she sliced across his throat before she could think. The gun in his hand clattered to the floor as the report of it going off echoed around the room. As she watched, in horror at what she'd done, his head rolled forward and bounced twice before coming to rest at her feet. The darkness swallowed her whole.

~~~

Carole wasn't sure what she was supposed to be doing. Grieving? Not likely. Should she be saddened about the death of her husband? She wasn't, and even thinking about it made her sick to her stomach. She had hated him for more years than she ever liked him, which wasn't all that long to begin with.

The police officer that had sat with her while the rest of them were questioned asked her if she was all right. Was she? She might be more all right than she'd ever been, but didn't say that to him.

"May I have a glass of something?" He stood up. "I know that it's still early, but I could use a glass of wine."

He nodded and left her. As she sat there trying her best to figure out what the heck she was going to do now, Linyah touched her mind.

They're saying that he had a massive heart attack. Anyone who knows him knows that he can be a stubborn man and he refused to acknowledge that he was dealing with a great deal of outside stress. She asked about his head not being attached to his body. *It was when they got here.*

They haven't arrested poor Hannah, have they? She's been through quite enough already. Linyah told her she wasn't being charged with anything. *Because of his heart attack. I see. What will the others say when questioned? Will they…what does Daniel say?*

He wanted me to ask you if you'd stay with him and Wanda for a time. He said that you have to deal with things when you return home, but for now, he'd like to visit with you. Hannah wants to get to know you as well.

Carole thought about it. She wanted to but…well, she wasn't even sure what to do when she got back to the big house. It had been in her family for more years than she could remember. She told her she'd think about it.

Her husband was dead. And she wasn't even sure what she should be feeling. Relief was at the forefront of her emotions, along with sadness at the way things had ended for him, and she was terrified. How would she function now? What would she do if someone asked her to join something again? There were times, a long time ago, when she'd been as social as any member of their friends. Then Kelli had left her, and she felt as if her world had become so small that she didn't want to move out of her corner for a long while. And while she'd been there, deep into her depression, her husband, already a monster, had become more of one, and then the abuse had become daily.

When someone sat next to her, she looked at Thomas and smiled. He was a good man, and she loved his wife as well. He handed her the glass of white wine, and she took a small sip before she spoke.

"I don't know what to do." He nodded, and she fought tears for a second before she continued. "He kept me locked away, away from people. He did so many...so very many horrible things to me that I don't know what to do now."

"You live." She nodded, knowing that it was easy for him to say. "It's not really. Easy for me. I have a mate that I'm much younger than...thousands of years younger. I have magic that seems to ooze from me that I have no idea how to control. I'm overwhelmed to the point of wanting to shift to my cat and run for hours, and maybe not returning, ever. Not as bad as losing a spouse, no, but still I can relate to feeling out of my element."

"I guess you can. Thousands of years?" Laughing, he told her yes. "I've never met anyone who looks so good to be that old. I'm assuming her parents...good heavens. They must be thousands older than that."

"Yes. They've been around for a very long time." He watched her for several seconds before he spoke again. "I would like to help you. I think—and this is only advice—I think you should move into the house that Hannah has purchased for you. Not forever, but long enough that the house out where you lived can be stripped of everything that was his and fresh paint put on the rooms. Your room should be made into something different...perhaps you could put a gym in there. Something that would not be what it was."

"I don't want to ever go back." Thomas smiled at her. "I know that I have to. There are things there, many things there that need to be dealt with. I have a business that I need to figure out what to do with. There is the money too. We had a great deal when we married, and I know that Howard was obsessed with having more. For all I know the entire company could be broke."

"It's not. You're very wealthy." She nodded. "And then there's the insurance money. You could live off that and never have to worry."

"I would like to provide for my family. I know that she doesn't need it, but I'd like to make sure that Hannah has everything she didn't have when growing up. To think that man knew where she was all this time. Do you suppose he knew how she'd suffered by that woman?" Thomas told her he more than likely did. "I do hate the man. I did before, but now...now I just want to go in there and shoot him. What a horrible thing to do to one of our children."

Thomas sat with her for a long while. He never yelled or screamed at her, never raised his fist to her or did any of the kind of things that Howard had done to her. Instead he answered her questions, advised when asked, and did something that no one had done for her in a very long time. He was her friend. When she felt as if she could deal with things again, she asked him if she could stay at the house that her granddaughter built her for a few nights.

"Just until I get my feet back under me. I know it's a great burden, but I'm not sure I want to be in a hotel." He stood up and when he left her, she thought for sure she was going to be arrested or something. Instead, both Daniel and Hannah came in. Carole pulled them both her and cried like a small child. She was so happy to have them that it took her a long time before she could speak to them.

"I just don't know how to tell you how sorry I am. I didn't know everything, but I should have guessed." Daniel told her about his wife, and she again had the urge to go find her dead husband and kill him again. The nerve of the man. Hannah simply held her hand and smiled a great deal.

After a little while, Daniel said he needed to take Wanda home, she wasn't feeling well. Hannah got up to pace and Carole's heart suffered for her. So while she worked out whatever it was she was walking off, Carole talked about Kelli.

"She was so very smart, my Kelli girl was. Top of her class in every subject. But she was stubborn too. I think you're a great deal like her in that respect." Hannah stopped moving and stared. "She dated this young man. His name was Pitmen. James Pitmen I think. He's dead now, I'm afraid. He'd been so depressed when he couldn't contact her, and when he'd come to the house asking about his Kelli, I had to turn him away. Sadly, he was killed in a robbery attempt. Not him as the robber, but as a person who just happened to be at the wrong place at the wrong time. He was smart too. James told me that he wanted to marry Kelli, but of course she'd been thrown out by her father and we never saw her again."

"Do you think your husband had anything to do with his death?" Carole had wondered the same thing over the years and had no idea. Telling Hanna that now seemed so wrong that she told her the only lie she promised herself she ever would.

"No. It was a robbery gone wrong." Hannah nodded and paced again. "You look a great deal like her. My Kelli. When I go back to the mansion, I'll send you some of her things. I had...there was a time when I had people in the house that would help me. I've hidden away some things that meant a great deal to me. And those were things of your mom's."

They talked until they were told they could leave. Misha came to get them and lead them out the back of the hotel instead of through the room where the body had been. When they were seated in the limo, Hannah finally asked her what had been bothering her.

"Will you forgive me for killing him?" Carole was shocked by the question and could only stare at Hannah with her mouth opened. "If I could do it over again, I'd take it back."

"You've done me the biggest favor in the world, child. I'm free. Free to love you the way I want and to get to know you. I'm very happy that he's gone from our lives. And you need to be as well." Hannah nodded and leaned against her husband. Carole smiled. "I think I'd very much like to take you up on the house, if you don't mind. I think I'd like to stay here until you're tired of me."

"You're welcome as long as you want." Misha nodded his agreement with his wife. Carole leaned back and closed her eyes. A new life, and she was so ready for it.

CHAPTER 13

Linyah stretched out on the bed. She'd not slept this well in a very long time. She supposed it was coming several dozen times that helped, but she did feel good. Thomas was still sleeping beside her, and she rolled over to look at him. He was so handsome that she found herself wanting to snap pictures of him all the time. And touch him. Watching him sleep, she wondered if she could have as much fun with his body as he'd had with hers, and looked down at his cock.

He wasn't as hard as he normally was when he was naked. But he was thick. She touched her finger over him, and he moaned. Linyah moved down the bed, slightly taking the sheet with her as she went. His cock was uncovered, and she found herself wanting to taste him as much as he had her. Leaning over him, she licked his length.

"Christ." His curse had her looking up at him, but his eyes were still closed. Licking him again, she moved her body so that she was between his legs and wrapped her hand around his hardening cock. Taking him into her mouth fully, she felt his hips move up and down as she tasted him. Linyah loved it when he fucked her mouth and bobbed up and down with him until she felt his fingers curl into her hair. This time when she looked up, he was staring right at her.

"Are you waking me this way every day?" She let go of his cock and smiled at him. "Don't stop now. I'm just waking up and enjoying this."

Linyah licked him from root to tip, then swallowed him down her throat. He roared out her name but didn't stop her. The more she took of him into her mouth, the harder he fucked her. When she was lifted from him and pulled up his body, Linyah started to beg him to let her go back and finish him when he told her to ride him. As she'd never done this before, it took her several tries to get it right.

"You're so beautiful right now." She rolled her hips forward, and he groaned again. "That's it, baby. Ride me. I love the feel of your tight pussy wrapped around me."

Thomas grabbed her hips to slow her down, but she didn't want to slow. She wanted a hard, fast ride. As she leaned forward, holding onto his chest as her climax built, she nearly came when he rolled her to her back. Instead of fucking her, he told her to lay still.

"I want you to shift." She shook her head. "Shift for me and go into the woods behind here. When I come after you, find you, I'm going to fuck you with my cat, then again as me."

"Fuck me now." He slid into her hard, then back out. "Yes. More. Please, give me what I want."

But he stopped again, and she wanted to scream at him. "Shift. Be a cat to mine. I want to claim you. Fuck you hard out in the open. Then if you're a good girl and let me mark you, I'll let my cat have a taste of your pussy again."

She watched him. She wasn't sure if he was teasing her or not, but when he pulled from her body, she leapt from the bed and let a leopard take her. The shift from human to an animal had never been her favorite thing, but with him, it seemed right. She moved to the door, and he followed. As he reached for the knob to let her out, she ran her tongue over his cock. She thought for sure he was going to shift then and take her, but he commanded her again to go into the woods. She was barely out of the house when she heard him coming for her.

Linyah ran like her life depended on it. He was always just behind her, and she wondered a couple of times if he was letting her get away. But each time she was able to elude him, he'd turn up very close to her again. Linyah wanted him to take her, but she was having a great deal of fun too.

Just when she thought she'd lost him again, he pounced and took her to the ground. He was deep within her in seconds.

Christ, you have no idea how much he's enjoyed this. She moaned, and her cat snarled at him. When his cat roared back, she tried to bite him, but he wasn't having it. Lifting her ass up to toss him off, he bit down into her shoulder so hard that she stilled.

He's marking you. Her cat hated what he was doing and tried again to toss him off. But he only bit her deeper until she lay still. The big cat pounded into her until he threw back his head and roared out his release.

She shifted back to herself almost as soon as he let her go. She lay there panting both from the fuck and the run. His cat moved around her as if he were cornering his prey. Linyah wasn't afraid, but she wasn't going to let him take her so easily.

Every time he got close enough to her, she moved back. He was pissed off; being denied what he wanted wasn't setting well with him. But when he lunged at her, throwing her back to the ground, he held her down with his big paws as he licked her breast. She watched him as he moved down her body, biting her enough to leave a mark but not enough to draw blood. As soon as he was at her pussy, she sat up on her elbows to watch him.

Let him in. She spread her legs for them both and waited. He was teasing her. She knew it and so did Thomas. But when his thick tongue touched her clit, she came with a quick, hard climax that left her breathless for more. As he licked her over and over, she began to ride his mouth. As soon as she felt her climax build again, she begged Thomas to take her.

The shift was fast, his body already in motion to move up, and his cock hard as stone. When he filled her, slammed his cock into her pussy, she let her climax take her. Screaming out her release, she held onto Thomas as he took her higher and higher twice more before she fell over the edge. Then he roared out his own climax. Hard punches of his body into hers brought her again. Linyah felt her body drop back to earth, almost as if he'd lifted her up to the heavens and dropped her back. Laying there while her heart seemed to pound out of her chest, she thought of how much she loved him.

He rolled to his back, taking her with him. Neither of them said a word as they lay there. It wasn't until he turned her head that she looked up. Not five feet from them was a big buck, but that wasn't all. Five of his harem were eating grass too.

"Do you suppose they saw us?" For some reason that made her embarrassed to think about. "I'm assuming you think they might have. What do you suppose they were thinking? 'Look honey, the humans are sticking things in each other again. How do they do that?'"

"Behave yourself." She giggled, and the buck looked at her. "I wonder if by this time next year he'll have a whole herd of baby deer."

"I would like to have children with you." She put her head on her fist and watched him now as he continued. "Not right away, I think. I'd like to spend some time getting to know you. Doing things with you."

"I love doing things to you." He grinned and slapped her ass. "Hey. That wasn't very nice. I was being serious."

He held her for a little while longer, and she closed her eyes. It was so peaceful there. The birds were making noises now. The deer that had been milling about them had moved on as well. There couldn't have been a more serene place in all of the world.

"I talked to your dad." She didn't move, waiting for him to ask her about it. Her dad told her that he didn't think that Thomas believed him. She smiled when she thought of his face when the ball, scheduled a month from now, was set to happen.

"He said you did. I guess you're not keen on being a prince." She felt his body stiffen but didn't move. "It really isn't that big of a deal. You get a crown, and you—"

Thomas rolled her to her back and put his hand over her mouth. She could see the panic in his eyes and had to work hard at not laughing at him. His mind was working, and she was very tempted to look inside, just to see how much he really was upset about this.

"There is a crown." She nodded. "And someone, I'm assuming your father, is going to put it on me."

She shook her head and since he didn't let her speak, she reached into his head and answered him. *My sister will. The queen rules in our society. The men help a great deal, but ultimately it's the queen's say.*

"I don't want this," Linyah said nothing, not sure what to tell him. "I've never been a prince before. Never held any title, for that matter. I simply don't want this."

Too bad. He let go of her mouth, and she looked at him. "I swear to you, it's just a title. You'll be asked to join a few things. Dad said he'd help you with that. But if it makes you feel any better, I will be the next in line only if Kendra wants to retire or anything."

"No, that does not make me feel better." He rolled to his back, this time not pulling her to him. "What the hell is my family going to say when they find out? Do you know what sort of shit they're going to give me?"

"Yes." He looked at her and she smiled. "But you can have them thrown in irons or whatever. You'll have an entire army at your command."

"Now that I can live with." He pulled her down over him and kissed her. "Let's go to bed. I want to make love to you again."

She was stretching out on their big bed when something else occurred to her. Linyah thought about telling him what she remembered, but decided to wait until the time was right. The poor man had enough on his plate right now. But when the crowning ceremony happened, he was going to have to make a speech. Linyah decided to help him with it. It was the least she could do.

About the Author

Kathi Barton, author of the bestselling series Force of Nature, lives in Nashport, Ohio with her husband Paul. In addition to writing full time Kathi likes to spend time with her eight grandkids, three children and three children-in-laws. She writes to relax and have fun.

Her muse, a cross between Jimmy Stewart and Hugh Jackman brings them to life for her readers in a way that has them coming back time and again for more. Her favorite genre is paranormal romance with a great deal of spice. You can visit Kathi on line and drop her an email if you'd like. She loves hearing from her fans. aaronskiss@gmail.com.

Follow Kathi on her blog:

http://kathisbartonauthor.blogspot.com/